The Sword,
The Ring,
and the Parchment

*An allegory
by Ed Dunlop*

(BOOK ONE IN THE TERRESTRIA CHRONICLES)

For ye have not received
the spirit of bondage again to fear;
but ye have received the
Spirit of adoption,
whereby we cry, Abba, Father.

The Spirit itself beareth witness with our spirit,
that we are the children of God;

And if children, then heirs;
heirs of God, and joint-heirs with Christ;
if so be that we suffer with him,
that we may be also glorified together.

– Romans 8: 15-17

Books by Ed Dunlop

The Terrestria Chronicles
The Sword, the Ring, and the Parchment
The Quest for Seven Castles
The Search for Everyman
The Crown of Kuros
The Dragon's Egg
The Golden Lamps

Jed Cartwright Adventure Series
The Midnight Escape
The Lost Gold Mine
The Comanche Raiders
The Lighthouse Mystery
The Desperate Slave
The Midnight Rustlers

The Young Refugees Series
Escape to Liechtenstein
The Search for the Silver Eagle
The Incredible Rescues

Sherlock Jones Detective Series
Sherlock Jones and the Assassination Plot
Sherlock Jones and the Willoughby Bank Robbery
Sherlock Jones and the Missing Diamond
Sherlock Jones and the Phantom Airplane
Sherlock Jones and the Hidden Coins
Sherlock Jones and the Odyssey Mystery

The 1,000-Mile Journey

Christian fiction: Ages 10 and up
www.dunlopministries.com
Cover Art by Laura Lea Sencabaugh and Wayne Coley

For the honor and glory
of my King

Introduction — The Land of Terrestria

Long, long ago, in a faraway land, there once was a peaceful kingdom known as Terrestria. It was a rugged land, with towering mountains, dense forests, and thundering waterfalls. It was a bountiful land, with bright meadows, abundant streams and rivers, and fertile soil. It was a prosperous, joyful land, for the people who inhabited the quiet villages and well-kept farms were ruled by the wise and powerful King Emmanuel. The people of Terrestria were happy and fulfilled, content in the knowledge that their King loved and cared for them.

But one day the storm clouds of trouble swept across the land. King Emmanuel's chief musician, a self-serving man by the name of Argamor, gathered a band of discontented subjects around him and led a revolt in a foolish attempt to seize King Emmanuel's throne. The insurrection failed. Argamor and the servants who had joined him were banished from the King's presence. Argamor fled to an obscure corner of the kingdom and became a blacksmith.

But Argamor still had plans to seize the throne. As the years of time marched on, he worked tirelessly to advance his own dominion, quietly gathering a secret army of servants who were disloyal to King Emmanuel. The wily blacksmith and his followers resided in a small town of rickety shacks and grimy shops that became known as the Village of Despair. Argamor worked day and night to enslave the minds, souls and hearts of the people in the hopes of one day seizing the throne of good King Emmanuel. Before long, every man, woman and child in the village wore heavy chains of slavery that had been forged in Argamor's miserable shop. His evil influence spread rapidly, and he soon claimed followers in many other towns and villages.

Thus, in time, the kingdom of Terrestria was divided, with many of the subjects loyal to King Emmanuel, while others blindly followed Argamor. Conflict was inevitable.

Chapter One

"Make haste, lad!" Argamor roared, looking up from the massive chain that he was fashioning on the anvil, his swarthy features twisted in anger. "You can work faster!"

The muscular arm of the huge blacksmith brought the heavy hammer down in a mighty blow against the glowing iron link upon the anvil, and the sound rang across the darkness of the November afternoon like a vesper bell. The man's lip curled in hatred as he watched the slender slave boy. Reaching up with a dirty hand to scratch his thick, black beard, he snarled, "You shall work harder, knave, or you shall taste the lash again!"

"Aye, my lord," young Josiah replied wearily. "I shall work faster, my lord." Gasping for breath, he struggled to haul the cumbersome coalscuttle across the muddy workyard. A freezing rain slashed at his back and the biting north wind sweeping down from the fells howled through his threadbare tunic, chilling his weary body. Reaching down with his free hand, Josiah grasped the heavy chain to relieve the weight of the iron shackle around his thin ankle. At the opposite end of the chain, a large iron ingot nearly half the boy's weight slid across the muddy ground.

The evil blacksmith chuckled as he held his hammer aloft,

pausing in his work to watch the feeble efforts of the boy. "The lad works hard," he said with a sneer. "Does he not, Evilheart?"

"Aye, that he does, my lord," Evilheart replied, fingering the lashes of his whip and stealing a quick glance at his companion, Lawofsin. "The lad does work hard."

"But he must be pushed to work harder!" Argamor roared, striking a ringing blow to the anvil. "The lad must learn to work faster!"

Argamor's two guards were as different from each other as two brothers could possibly be. Evilheart was clearly a descendant of the Early Kings—a stout bulldog of a man, with arms and shoulders so thick that it appeared as if he had no neck. With his shaved head and stern countenance, he struck fear into Josiah's heart every time he came near. Lawofsin, while of the same heritage, was tall and lanky, with muscles like ropes and a mournful, melancholy expression on his thin face. He had a huge shock of unruly brown hair that was always in need of washing. Both men carried whips. Josiah was almost as afraid of the two guards as he was of their master.

Struggling against the weight of the chain and the scuttle heaped with large chunks of coal, Josiah had managed to reach the shelter of the shed. Dragging the weight of guilt across the stone floor, he approached the edge of the flaming forge and timidly moved within arm's reach of his burly master. The forge was an open furnace nearly three yards across with a huge bellows mounted at one side. By pumping air with the bellows, Argamor could heat the forge until it was hot enough to turn iron cherry-red.

Setting the scuttle on the rock ledge at the edge of the forge, Josiah stepped up onto the ledge to empty his burden of coal into the glowing furnace. Smoke and heat from the forge billowed around him, burning his eyes and searing his lungs. The blistering heat of the open fire was worse than the cold and rain outside. Josiah took a deep breath and struggled to lift the clumsy scuttle to the red-hot lip of the forge.

"Faster, lad!" The unexpected blow across the back knocked Josiah off balance, nearly sending him into the flames. His heart pounded as he struggled to keep from tumbling forward. He threw out one hand to regain his balance, touched the edge of the forge, and recoiled with a howl of pain.

Argamor and his two henchmen roared with laughter.

Tears filled Josiah's eyes. "I-I can't work any faster, my lord," he stammered, struggling to keep his voice from trembling. Turning his face to avoid the worst of the heat, he emptied the coal into the blazing forge while sparks from the fire leaped upwards and swirled around his head like glowing fireflies.

"And why not?" Argamor roared. "You *must* work faster!" The hammer crashed down on the anvil with a thunderous impact that made Josiah flinch.

"I've been working hard all day, my lord," the boy replied fearfully, cringing at the prospect of a sudden fist. "I haven't eaten since this morning, my lord, and I'm hungry, and tired, and cold."

"Are you complaining?" The blacksmith's cruel face contorted with rage and his dark eyes glittered with fury. Having completed his work on the huge chain, he hurled it onto an enormous pile of other chains.

"Nay, my lord," Josiah replied hastily. Gripping his own chain, he dragged the weight of guilt across the floor and moved away from the huge man. "But if you would remove the chain of iniquity and the weight of guilt from my ankle, I could work faster, my lord."

Argamor threw back his head and roared with heartless laughter. "Remove the chain? Evilheart, did you hear the lad? He wants me to remove his chain!" The blacksmith stepped closer to Josiah. His black beard framed yellow, twisted teeth as he flashed a leering grin. "You want me to remove your chain, lad? So you can make your escape?"

Fear washed over the youth as the man moved closer. "Nay, my lord. But methinks that if you were to remove the weight of guilt, I could work harder."

Argamor loomed over Josiah and a sulphurous stench overpowered the youth, choking and gagging him. "The chain is your own, lad, of your own making. Your worthy master would never consider taking it from you. The weight of guilt is yours and yours alone." He smiled. "It is yours forever."

"But the chain is heavy, my lord, and the shackle chafes against my ankle. It hurts me so! And the weight of guilt slows me down and drains my strength as I drag it everywhere I go." Trembling with exhaustion, Josiah sank to a sitting position on the warm stone of the ledge. The empty coalscuttle clattered to the stone floor.

Argamor was enraged. "Stand to your feet!" he roared. "Do you presume to slack in the very presence of your master?" A huge fist struck Josiah on the shoulder.

Josiah stood wearily, fearfully snatching the scuttle from the floor where it had fallen. "I beg pardon, sire. I am weary, and I am hungry, and I am wet and cold. I cannot carry on, sire. I must rest."

The angry blacksmith leaped forward and seized the boy. Lifting him by one arm and one leg, he hoisted him high into the air so that the weight of guilt swung freely at the end of its chain, causing the shackle to bite painfully into Josiah's ankle. "You are cold, are you?" Argamor roared. Snarling with rage, he held the trembling youth over the glowing, pulsating forge. "If I drop you in, you will no longer be cold!"

Josiah was terrified. The heat from the forge blistered his arms and face, singeing his eyebrows and burning his throat. He gasped for breath. If the master should release his grip, he would drop helplessly into the hungry, crackling flames...

"Not another word of complaint, churlish knave, or I shall cast you in," Argamor growled, hurling the boy to the floor beside the forge. "Get back to work!"

Sobbing helplessly, Josiah retrieved his coalscuttle, grasped his chain with his free hand, and crept from the shed into the onslaught of cold rain. His bare foot splashed into a chilling puddle, but he barely noticed. His heart ached. Why, oh why, must Argamor be so cruel? Was he not doing his best? What more could a master ask of a slave? Was there to be no relief from the constant, backbreaking work, the sting of the lash, the cruel mocking of Argamor and his henchmen, Evilheart and Lawofsin? Was the wicked blacksmith correct—were the chain of iniquity and the weight of guilt to be his forever?

Lightning slashed across the blackness of the afternoon sky and the thunder boomed angrily in reply. The wind howled and shrieked like a living creature agonizing in pain as the chilling rain pummeled the helpless slave boy. Back bowed against the unrelenting weight at the end of the chain, Josiah slogged wearily through the mud for another load of coal. A moaning sob escaped his trembling lips. "Is there to be no escape from this misery?" he cried softly. "Must I wear this chain and serve this wretched man forever? Is there no one to care?"

Chapter Two

Josiah's heart pounded against his ribs like a hammer upon the anvil as he stood breathlessly beside the crackling forge. Hardly daring to breathe, the boy slowly tugged at his chain, pulling the weight of guilt cautiously across the rough stones of the floor. Reaching Argamor's huge iron anvil, he paused and looked around anxiously. The master had stepped from the shed for a moment, and Evilheart and Lawofsin had turned their backs. No one was watching.

The blacksmith's file lay on the workbench beside the anvil, Josiah's for the taking. The boy had seen Argamor use the tool to shape various projects, and he knew that it would cut iron. Dare he take it? Dare he risk the fury of Argamor, should the blame fall upon him, as it surely must? He shook his head. The risk was too great.

But then again, if he dared, and if he succeeded in the theft, would not the rewards be worth the danger he would have placed himself in? The file could be used to cut iron—why not iron bars? The simple tool, placed carelessly beside the anvil by the cruel blacksmith, was to Josiah the very symbol of freedom.

He held his breath, listening intently, watching Evilheart and

Lawofsin closely. The deed would just take a moment—one step closer to the anvil, a lightning-quick snatch, and the precious file would be safely hidden away inside his tunic. Hardly daring to breathe, he inched closer.

Crack! A chunk of coal in the forge flew apart with a loud snap, startling him and causing him to jump in fright. Wilting in disappointment, he took a step away from the anvil and the file. The risk was simply too great—if Argamor discovered him with the tool, he would be beaten unmercifully. He couldn't take the chance.

But the dream of freedom nudged him forward, causing him to step toward the workbench again. The file lay before him like a precious treasure, tempting and tantalizing in its nearness, unrelenting in its appeal. The tool seemed to call to him. "Take me! I can grant you freedom! Freedom! I can set you free!"

Josiah stepped closer. His mind was made up; the risks were enormous, but he would take the file. He struggled to will himself to reach for the tool, but found that he was paralyzed with fear. His hand simply wouldn't obey.

He glanced toward the doorway of the blacksmith shed where Evilheart and Lawofsin stood looking out across the rainy workyard. He took a deep breath. It was now or never. If he was to take the precious file, he had to act quickly. Argamor could return at any instant.

Grimacing in fear, Josiah reached for the file. His heart leaped as his fingers closed around it. The tool was his! He snatched it from the workbench and thrust it inside his tunic, wincing as the end of the file scraped his ribs.

"What are you doing?" The words cut through the stillness like a clap of thunder.

Argamor stood framed in the opening of the shed, his huge bulk silhouetted against a sky lit by a white-hot bolt of lightning. Josiah recoiled in panic. He had been caught! Argamor had seen him steal the file, and now he would experience the full wrath of the cruel blacksmith. "My lord, I—I..." Josiah stammered. His voice failed him as terror overwhelmed him. He trembled like a leaf in a windstorm.

Argamor snatched the whip from the grasp of Evilheart and strode forward furiously. "Don't just stand there, you idle little wretch!" the man snarled. "Get to work!" The whip lashed out like a venomous serpent to bite Josiah on the arm. Argamor raised the whip again.

Josiah lunged for the coalscuttle, snatched it up, and bolted for the doorway, dragging the chain and weight behind him with an energy that he never knew that he possessed. He pushed his way past Evilheart and Lawofsin to escape into the safety of the cold outside. The whip made a whooshing sound as it cut through the air to strike Evilheart instead of Josiah. The guard gave a startled howl of pain. "Keep working!" Argamor raged, screaming curses at Josiah. "You must never stand idle!"

The boy dragged the scuttle and the weight of guilt across the muddy workyard and gave a tremendous sigh of relief. Argamor hadn't seen the theft, after all. He hurried to the coal pile, and, working furiously, began to load the heavy chunks into the scuttle. As he worked, his fear began to subside and his heart ceased its frantic pounding. The file was his! Tonight he would begin work on the one thing that mattered most—escape. It might take several nights' work to cut through the bars of his cell, but one day soon he would be free of the hated Argamor. He would taste the sweet nectar of freedom!

Josiah dropped a huge chunk of coal into the scuttle, and, glancing furtively around to ascertain that he was not being watched, reached quickly inside his tunic. The file lay against his belly, safely hidden in the folds of the tunic. He pushed the file into place more securely and continued with the loading.

The gloomy daylight had faded and darkness had descended upon the Village of Despair when Argamor placed his hammer upon his anvil and strode toward the door of the shop. "See that the lad is secured in his cell," he ordered the two guards. "We start work again at daybreak."

Evilheart and Lawofsin both bowed low. "As you wish, my lord," Evilheart replied. "It shall be done." The hardhearted blacksmith disappeared into the blackness of the night.

"Come, knave," Lawofsin demanded, shoving Josiah forward and laughing when the boy stumbled over his chain. "It's time to return to your cell." He led Josiah outside to a garbage pile in the alleyway behind the shed. "Make haste," he said impatiently.

Josiah sank to his knees in the garbage and rested for a moment. Feeling cautiously about in the darkness, he found a rotting apple and a few cabbage leaves. "Make haste, knave," Lawofsin demanded.

"It's dark, sire," Josiah replied. "It's hard to see anything."

"You have had ample time," the guard replied curtly. "Come along." Josiah had no choice but to follow, clutching his chain in one hand and his meager findings in the other.

Lawofsin led him through the narrow, filthy streets of the darkened Village of Despair, stopping before the imposing iron gate of the Dungeon of Condemnation. He rapped on the iron bars with the wooden handle of his whip and then waited impatiently. Moments later a light flickered faintly in the darkness of the corridor. Footsteps echoed throughout the dark passageway and a helmeted guard carrying a lighted torch rounded a corner and approached the gate with a huge ring of keys in his hand.

"Heartless," Josiah's escort greeted the guard, "are you on duty tonight?"

"Tonight and every night," Heartless replied in a dismal voice. "I've been stationed here by his highness, Lord Argamor. The Dungeon of Condemnation is now my station, I fear." A key turned in the lock and the heavy gate swung open.

"The lad is your responsibility," Lawofsin declared, and then disappeared into the darkness of the street.

Knowing that it was useless to do otherwise, Josiah dragged his weight of guilt through the gate, and Heartless locked the iron barrier behind him. The prison guard held his torch high and led the way down the dank corridor. Dragging his weight of guilt behind him, Josiah followed meekly. Josiah dropped his eyes as they walked along, disheartened by the sight of the pitiful wretches imprisoned within the cells on each side of the dimly lit corridor.

Together they passed down a flight of crumbling steps and through another locked gate. Heartless paused before an empty cell, selected a key from his ring, and unlocked the door. Without a word, Josiah stepped inside. The familiar feeling of hopelessness engulfed the lonely boy as Heartless locked the door and turned away. Hopelessness turned to despair as the flickering light from the torch disappeared down the passageway.

Josiah crept to the rear of the cell and dropped wearily to his knees in a pile of filthy straw. He let the apple and the cabbage leaves fall into the straw. The cell was dark and dismal; the only light in the tiny chamber came from the sputtering torch at the far end of the cellblock. Water seeped down the cold stone wall and formed a little puddle in one corner before draining out through a crack in the floor. Sensing movement out of the corner of his eye, Josiah turned in time to see a large rat dash across the floor and disappear through a drain hole. He shuddered. The worst part of servitude to Argamor had always been the long nights of despair spent alone in the Dungeon of Condemnation.

But tonight was different; Josiah had a ray of hope. With a sigh of expectancy, he drew the stolen file from the bosom of his tunic and studied it. Unable to properly examine the tool in the dim light, Josiah crept silently to the bars at the front of his cell and held the file up to the torchlight. Five letters were engraved in the handle of the file: W-O-R-K-S. The letters were foreign and meaningless to the illiterate slave boy, but he sensed that somehow they were of great significance. Perhaps this was the key to freedom from the Dungeon of Condemnation!

He paused to listen carefully. The dungeon was silent. Holding his breath, he placed the edge of the file down low against the bar at the farthest corner of his cell and drew it gently across the cold iron. The file made a faint screeching noise and Josiah winced. He would have to be cautious; if he filed too vigorously and made too much noise, his plans for escape would be discovered!

His meager supper was forgotten as he set to work. Gripping the file at both ends to minimize the noise, Josiah drew the pilfered tool back and forth repeatedly across the cold iron of the prison bar. Back and forth, back and forth. The file whined softly as it sped to and fro across the iron. The lonely boy experienced a surge of new energy as he contemplated the details of his escape. Once he had cut through the cell bar, he would leave it in place so that the guards would not discover his efforts. He realized that the project would undoubtedly take several nights, but he was ready for that.

The problem would come when he attempted to cut through the door to the cellblock. Once he bent the bar to exit from his cell, he would have to complete his escape from the prison the same night, for the damaged bar would surely be discovered the next morning. But there would be no way that he could hope to cut through the door in one night—what was he to do?

I'll have several days to think about it, he told himself, *while I work on this bar.* Pausing to examine his progress, he felt the bar with an exploratory fingernail and was dismayed to find that he had barely scratched the iron. *This is going to take longer than I thought.*

Placing the file carefully against the scratch mark, he resumed work on the obstinate iron bar. Back and forth, back and forth. *This is going to take a thousand thousand strokes!* He sighed at the thought.

Hearing a slight noise in the corridor, Josiah glanced up and was dismayed to see a shadowy figure standing less than five paces from his cell! He had been so intent upon his work that he had not been alert enough to hear the man approaching. His heart sank. His plans for escape were about to be discovered!

The figure approached the cell and Josiah was surprised to see a small golden cross suspended from a golden chain about the man's neck. The feeble light from the cellblock torch glittered on the polished surface of the relic. The man's shaved head and floor-length broadcloth robe confirmed Josiah's identity of the visitor. This was a man of the Church.

"Friend," the cleric whispered, gripping the bars of Josiah's cell with both hands, "would you find freedom from the confines of the Dungeon of Condemnation?"

It took Josiah a moment to figure out the meaning of the unexpected visitor's words. "Aye," he said eagerly, when he realized that the cleric was asking if he wanted to escape from the dungeon. "Aye, my lord, I desire that more than life itself!"

"I am Father Almsdeeds, a man of the Church," the cleric whispered gently. "I have the keys that will free you from this dreadful abode. Here—take them. This is the Key of Religion," he explained, passing a shiny golden key through the bars to his young beneficiary, "and this is the Key of Penance." He handed a second key through the bars.

Josiah was ecstatic. "Will these really get me out?" he asked eagerly.

"Aye, my son," the cleric assured him softly. "These two, and this third one, the Key of Sincerity, will open the doors to freedom from condemnation." After whispering these words, he passed a third key through the bars.

"I thank you," Josiah whispered gratefully. "You have brought me hope in this lonely dungeon of despair."

"It is my privilege," the stealthy visitor assured him. "Go in peace, and may the blessings of the Church brighten your path forever." The shiny cross swung back and forth as the man turned away.

"Wait!" Josiah whispered urgently.

Father Almsdeeds turned back to face him.

"What about my chain of iniquity and my weight of guilt? How must I remove those?"

The cleric seemed perplexed by the question. "You must take them with you," he replied haltingly, as if unsure that he was giving the correct response. "Perhaps once you are free of these confines, another can help you remove your chain." Giving Josiah a shrug and a bewildered look, he turned and hurried away.

Josiah's heart was filled with joy and expectation as he tossed the stolen file upon the pile of straw and turned his attention to the three keys. Holding them up to the feeble light from the torch, he discovered to his amazement that all three were encrusted with glittering jewels. The exceptional beauty of the golden keys made his heart pound faster.

Listening for a moment to determine that all was quiet, he crept eagerly to the door of his cell and inserted a key in the lock. The key slid in easily. He took a deep breath. His heart pounded with anticipation. He gently twisted the golden key, which turned easily in the lock. To his dismay, nothing happened. Frowning with disappointment, he twisted the key in the opposite direction—one full turn, and then two, and finally, three. Still, nothing happened. The cell door was as tightly locked as ever.

I have used the wrong key, he told himself, withdrawing the golden key from the lock. *Perhaps this is the Key of Sincerity, and I should have used the Key of Penance or the Key of Religion. This key must fit the lock on the outer gate.*

Placing the first key carefully inside his tunic, he slowly

inserted a second into the lock. He twisted gently, but the result was the same. The key turned easily, but the door was still locked.

He tried the third key, again with no success.

Hours later, Josiah was still standing wearily at the cell door, still trying vainly to open the lock. He tried each of the three golden keys repeatedly, twisting first one way and then another, but the door remained locked. Finally, he sank to his knees in exhausted frustration, dropping the beautiful Keys of Religion, Penance and Sincerity to the cold stone floor.

"Father Almsdeeds must have given me the wrong keys," he said with a sigh of despair. "I'm still the prisoner of Argamor, and these keys have accomplished nothing!" Gripping the bars of the cell door, he shook them with all his might. But the door was unyielding; the cell was still locked. Refusing to admit defeat, Josiah carefully picked up the golden keys and resumed work on the lock.

Daylight had already crept over the eastern wall of the Dungeon of Condemnation when the disheartened boy finally realized the futility of the golden keys given to him by Father Almsdeeds. He had worked all night; he had done his best; but the cell door was still securely locked. The Keys of Religion, Penance and Sincerity had accomplished nothing. Hiding the glittering keys and the stolen file under the pile of flea-infested straw, Josiah sank to the floor in utter defeat.

Chapter Three

"Arise, knave! Be up and about!" A booted foot struck Josiah in the ribs, and he opened his eyes to find Heartless glaring fiercely down at him. "Arise, wretched dog! Your master awaits!"

Groaning with weariness, the boy rolled over on his belly and rose stiffly to his knees. He yawned. The long, sleepless night had taken its toll. He was tired, so thoroughly exhausted that he could scarcely function, and yet the day was just starting and he knew that he faced long hours of relentless toil and abuse.

"Here." Heartless thrust a stoneware vessel into his hands, a bowl containing a thin, cold barley gruel. Knowing that it was to be his only sustenance that day, Josiah hurriedly gulped the watery, tasteless substance. When he finished, the guard snatched the vessel from his hands and hurled it into the corridor.

"Come." Heartless stepped from the cell and stood impatiently in the dimly lit corridor. Josiah rose slowly to his feet, grabbed his chain of iniquity with both hands, and dragged the heavy weight of guilt across the rough stones. The cell door slammed shut behind him. Josiah followed the prison guard up the stairs.

Lawofsin was waiting at the main gate of the Dungeon of Condemnation. "There's the worthless wretch," he said, when he saw Josiah. He stared searchingly at the boy. "Your eyes are red and your countenance is pale," he declared harshly. "Did you not sleep?"

"Perchance the lad stayed awake all night contemplating his escape plan," Heartless said with a sneer, and both men laughed.

Josiah stared at the prison guard. Panic rose within his breast. *He doesn't know,* he tried to tell himself. *Surely he doesn't know! No one saw me take the file! But what if he knows about Father Almsdeeds' visit to my cell? What if he knows about the golden keys?* Alarmed, he studied the man's face, trying desperately to determine if Heartless knew what had transpired during the night. But the guard's face was impassive, and Josiah learned nothing.

Rusty hinges screeched in protest as the prison gate swung open. "Come, knave," Lawofsin demanded, cuffing Josiah on the shoulder. "Lord Argamor will be angry if you are delayed."

The burly blacksmith had already fired the forge and was working at his anvil when Lawofsin thrust Josiah roughly through the doorway of the shed. Argamor looked up in irritation as the boy fell heavily to the stone floor. "Worthless knave," the blacksmith snarled, "get up and get working! You are behind in your duties!" Snatching an iron fragment from his workbench, he hurled it at Josiah, striking the boy in the shoulder.

Josiah blinked back tears as he rose to his feet and reached for the battered handle of the coalscuttle. "Aye, my lord," he answered feebly. "I ask your pardon, my lord." Argamor ignored him and turned his attention to the huge iron chain that he was fashioning on the anvil.

I cannot go on in this manner, Josiah told himself, dragging his heavy chain with one hand and carrying the empty coalscuttle in the other. *I cannot serve Argamor any longer! There must be a way to escape—there has to be!* He reached the coal pile, dropped his chain, and began to load the heavy chunks into the scuttle with both hands. *If I can just make it through today, I will sleep for a little while and then use Argamor's file to cut through the bar. It may take several days, but I will escape! I have to!*

He paused with a chunk of coal in his hands as he thought about the golden keys given to him by Father Almsdeeds. *Why did they not work?* he asked himself. *I wore myself out trying the keys—but in vain. I am still the slave of Lord Argamor!* Lawofsin stepped from the shed at that moment, and Josiah set aside his thoughts and worked faster.

The day was long. Weakened by the lack of sleep, Josiah was exhausted before mid-morning. Struggling to keep his eyes open, the boy stumbled frequently, often dropping his scuttle and spilling his load of coal. Each and every time, Argamor or one of his henchmen rewarded the weary boy with the stinging lash of the whip.

Daylight was fading rapidly as Josiah wearily carried the coalscuttle to the coal pile for yet another load. When he reached the pile, he suddenly sank to the ground, overcome with fatigue. He struggled to rise to his feet, but found that he no longer had the strength to do so. He watched the shed anxiously. If Argamor or one of the guards should see him resting, the beating that resulted would be unbearable. Gripping a huge chunk of coal with both hands, Josiah made a valiant effort to stand. He grunted with the effort as he did his best to pull himself to a standing position, but found that he could not. His strength was gone.

He managed to raise himself up on his knees. Resting his right forearm on the rim of the coalscuttle for support, he loaded small pieces of coal with his left hand. He watched the shed fearfully, terrified that his cruel master would appear at any instant.

He reached for another piece of coal. *Why didn't Father Almsdeeds' keys work last night?* he asked himself again. *Should I try them again tonight, or should I work on the bars with Argamor's file? One thing for certain—I must get some sleep tonight before I do anything!*

His thoughts went back to that day so long ago when he had first met the cruel blacksmith on the streets of the Village of Despair. A gang of beggar boys had set out to thrash Josiah for intruding on their territory when a huge man with a thick beard had stepped in and saved the frightened orphan from a beating. After chasing the gang of beggars away, the man had turned to Josiah with a warm smile. "Do you not have a home, lad?"

"Nay, my lord," Josiah replied, trembling with fear.

Argamor had seemed so friendly, almost caring, when he said, "I am a blacksmith, lad, and I am called by the name Argamor. Why not come and work for me? You shall have plenty of food and a dry place to sleep. The work is not hard, and I will pay you generous wages. There will be plenty of time for merriment; you can do whatever you want. What do you say, lad— would you be my apprentice?"

And so the trusting little boy had eagerly followed the big man with the friendly smile and the promises of a better life. At first, the work had not been hard and Josiah had been treated quite well. Argamor fed him three times a day, allowed him to sleep on a straw pallet at the rear of the shop, and even handed him a silver coin or two from time to time. At first, life with Argamor was pleasant for the little orphan boy.

Josiah shuddered as he remembered the day that Argamor had fastened the shackle around his ankle, explaining that it was only temporary and would soon be removed. And then, day by day, one link at a time, the chain had been added, and finally, the weight of guilt. On the evening that the weight of guilt had been fastened to Josiah's ankle he had also been locked in the Dungeon of Condemnation for the first time. The terrible beatings had started the very next day.

He sighed. How long it had taken him to realize that Argamor was his tormentor, rather than his benefactor! The life of merriment that the blacksmith had promised had quickly turned into a life of misery and cruelty.

Josiah struggled to his feet. The scuttle was only half-full, but he didn't have the strength to lift it. He strained to drag it across the workyard. After a several minutes of arduous effort, he neared the shed. Pausing to catch his breath, he heard the voice of Evilheart from within the structure.

"The lad is hardly more than a skeleton, my lord," Evilheart said in the tone of voice one would use when appealing to a great monarch.

"What concern is that of mine?" Argamor's voice was cold and disinterested. The hammer rang against the anvil with a steady rhythm.

"Perhaps, sire, you are driving the lad too hard."

The sound of the hammer ceased for several long seconds. "He's my slave; I'll do as I please with him." The hammer struck the anvil again.

"But my lord, the lad is ready to perish. We give him less than a pauper's portion of gruel in the morning, and allow him less than five minutes to scavenge the garbage pit at night. What if you were to give the lad a little more food?" Evilheart's voice faltered at that point, and Josiah surmised that he must have gotten a negative reaction from Argamor. "Perchance you gave the lad one or two brief rest periods during the day—would not he then able to work that much harder for you?"

"Rest periods?" The words came out as an indignant snarl.

"Brief ones, my lord. Perhaps even just one a day." Evilheart was losing ground, and he knew it. His tone was conciliatory, almost apologetic.

"Why should I?" Argamor's voice was flat and apathetic. The hammer was silent.

"Watching the lad, my lord, methinks that he is ready to die."

"If he dies, he dies," Argamor replied. "I simply get another slave—it matters not to me. Now, not another word about more food or rest periods!" The hammer clattered to the floor. "I'm through for the day. Take the lad to the dungeon. Speak not to me again concerning rest periods or more food."

"Aye, my lord."

Overcome with fatigue, Josiah sagged against the wall of the shed, still clutching his coalscuttle. Argamor strode from the shed and brushed past him, apparently not even seeing him.

"So why do you care for the lad?" Lawofsin asked Evilheart.

"You took up for him as if he were your little brother." Josiah was wondering the same thing, and he waited for Evilheart's answer.

"The lad means nothing to me," Evilheart told his companion. "But if he dies, his work might fall to me. And besides, better treatment of the lad might mean better treatment for us."

Josiah's body shook with a racking cough. Mustering his strength, he hefted the coalscuttle and entered the shed, dragging the hated chain and weight behind him. Argamor's two guards looked at him sternly. "It's time to return to your cell," Lawofsin said gruffly. He peered into the half-full scuttle. "Your work is found wanting, you worthless churl. You must do better tomorrow."

It was well past midnight when Josiah stirred from his pile of moldy straw. He listened intently for several moments to be certain that no one else was present in the cellblock and then retrieved his file from its hiding place under the straw. Silently he crept toward the corner of his cell. His heart pounded with anticipation—tonight was the night. It had taken eight nights to file his way through the iron bar, and tonight he would finish the job. Fully aware that he could never hope to cut his way through the gate in just one night, he had finally decided that was the purpose for which Father Almsdeeds' golden keys were intended.

Kneeling beside the prison bar on which he had already spent so many hours, he carefully placed the edge of the file against the deep notch in the iron and resumed his attack on the barrier. He had already cut a deep notch in the upper end of the bar to weaken it—cutting on the back side so that the cut would not be visible to any guards passing by—so that once the bottom was severed the entire bar would easily bend out of place.

The file grew hot as he worked relentlessly at the iron. Back and forth, back and forth, steadily sawing away at the bar that stood between him and freedom. "Freedom! Freedom! Freedom!" the rhythm of the file seemed to chant. Within hours, he would be free of the Dungeon of Condemnation. The thought gave him new strength and determination, and the file cut through the iron even faster than it had before.

Two hours later, Josiah felt like shouting when the stolen tool finally cut through the last fragment of iron. Placing the file quietly on the cold stone floor, Josiah grasped the bar with both hands and strained upward with all of his might. To his delight, the iron bent easily out of place.

He sprang across the cell toward the straw pile, pausing in consternation when his momentum jerked the chain of iniquity across the stone with a terrible clanking sound that echoed throughout the dank corridor. Carefully he pulled the chain taut and dragged the weight of guilt across the cell as noiselessly as possible. Kneeling at the straw pile, he quickly retrieved the three precious keys and tucked them inside his tunic along with Argamor's file.

Moments later Josiah wriggled through the space he had created between the bars. His heart was in his throat as he carefully pulled the weight of guilt out into the corridor. He stood to his feet and a feeling of exhilaration swept over him. He had done it! He had escaped from his cell!

Dragging the weight of guilt as quietly as he could, Josiah made his way down the dimly lit corridor. He paused before the iron gate and fumbled for the golden keys. He selected a key at random and inserted it into the lock. To his amazement, the gate swung slowly open even before he attempted to turn the key!

He hesitated for a moment, listening intently. The Dungeon of Condemnation was deathly quiet. Slowly, carefully, he pushed the gate open wider and crept through. He turned and pulled the weight of guilt through after him, wincing as the ingot slid across the stones with a harsh grating noise. Closing the gate noiselessly behind him, he headed for the stairs that led to the upper level.

Footsteps echoed in the corridor, and panic seized him. He was about to be discovered! Glancing wildly about, he was terror-stricken to realize that there was no convenient hiding place. There wasn't time to attempt to return to his cell, and the sound of the weight against the cobblestones would be a dead giveaway if he tried. Not knowing what else to do, he dropped to the floor at the foot of the stairs.

The footsteps came closer. Josiah waited in terror. His stomach tightened, and his body began to tremble. The blood pounded in his head. His chest felt so tight that he could scarcely breathe. Paralyzed with fear, he knew that he was completely helpless. If they found him, they might as well kill him on the spot. Argamor would show him no mercy.

The figure of a guard appeared in the darkness of the corridor, strode straight toward him, and then turned the corner less than fifteen paces from him. The sound of the man's footsteps receded as he disappeared down the other passageway. Josiah let out his breath in a grateful sigh of relief.

The trembling boy waited at the foot of the stairs for several moments, afraid to move lest the guard should suddenly reappear. When some time had passed and all was still quiet, he rose to his feet and cautiously dragged the weight of iniquity to the edge of the first step. Standing atop the step, he gripped the chain of iniquity with both hands and attempted to pull the weight up onto the stair.

It was then that Josiah discovered that his escape was not to be as easy as it had seemed. He pulled with all his might, but the heavy weight refused to budge. In his weakened condition, he could not lift the weight of guilt up the stairs! He gripped the chain down lower, closer to the weight, and tried again. Taking a deep breath, he threw every ounce of his strength into the effort, but the heavy weight would not move. He simply did not have the strength to pull the weight of guilt up the steep stairs.

Disheartened, he dropped to a sitting position on the second stair and pondered his predicament. His mind jumped back to that morning, when Heartless had led him from his dungeon cell. He suddenly realized that the guard had grabbed his chain and pulled the weight up the stairs for him. *How many times has he done that?* Josiah wondered. *Here I am, growing steadily weaker, and I didn't even realize it!*

He stood to his feet. *I must pull the weight up these stairs! I have to!* Gripping the chain with renewed vigor, he pulled with everything he had. But it simply wasn't enough. The weight wasn't going anywhere.

The file! I can cut the chain with the file! I need to be free of the weight of guilt anyway; I can't drag it all the way to freedom. Dropping to his knees, Josiah pulled the file from his tunic and set to work.

The file made a dreadful scraping, screeching sound when Josiah drew it across the first link in the chain. He stopped, panic-stricken, expecting the guards to come running. His heart pounded with fear as he waited in tense silence. But the dungeon was silent; no guards appeared. Apparently, the noise had not been as loud as he had imagined.

Holding the chain against the side of his leg to muffle the sound, Josiah again drew the file carefully across the link. There! That was much better! The screech of the file was not nearly as loud. Encouraged, he set to work in earnest. Watching the corridor and listening for footsteps, he filed furiously at the chain of iniquity.

He worked steadily for a long while without stopping. The file seemed to fly back and forth across the iron link. Metal shavings flew this way and that, and he knew that he was making excellent progress. The chain would be severed within minutes! His heart was light as he thought of the blessed relief that freedom from the chain of iniquity and the weight of guilt would bring.

After a prolonged period of energetic work on the chain, Josiah stopped to evaluate his progress. Switching the file to his left hand, he ran a finger over the link on which he had been working. He snatched his hand away. The chain was hot!

He leaned over sideways for a look at the chain. He stared, unable to believe his eyes. It was all he could do to hold back a cry of frustration. The chain was still intact! In spite of all his work, it wasn't even scratched. His determined efforts hadn't accomplished anything!

But I saw metal shavings, he told himself. *If the file isn't cutting through the chain, where did those come from?*

With a sinking feeling in the pit of his stomach, he knew the answer even before he looked. He held Argamor's file up to the dim light and examined it. Just as he had feared, he found that the tool was nearly worn in two. The file was not cutting the chain of iniquity; the chain was wearing out the file!

He bowed his head in defeat. "It's hopeless," he whispered aloud. "I just can't do this! Unless someone helps me, there's no escape! I'll be a prisoner in the Dungeon of Condemnation forever!" Tears flowed down his cheeks and dripped from his chin to spatter on the dirty floor.

Hearing a slight noise, Josiah raised his head to find two dungeon guards staring down at him. "Going somewhere, knave?" the taller one growled fiercely.

Chapter Four

"You are mine!" Argamor raged, screaming in fury. He snatched his hammer from his anvil and hurled it suddenly at Josiah. The boy ducked as the heavy tool sailed past his head and struck the wall behind him. "You are mine—do you hear me? Mine! I can do anything that I please with you, wretched dog! You are mine forever! I can kill you, banish you to the dungeon forever, or do anything I please with you! Do you not understand that?"

Josiah cowered before his furious master. "Aye, my lord."

"And yet you have attempted an escape?"

Terrified, Josiah simply dropped his gaze. The life seemed to go out of him and he swayed as though he was going to fall, but Evilheart and Lawofsin grabbed his arms and supported him.

"Answer me!!"

"Aye, my lord." Josiah's reply came out as a terrified little squeak.

"Why?"

"I-I simply can't bear to live the way I do, my lord. I work from daybreak until nightfall each day with hardly enough food to keep a mouse alive. I sleep in a cold, wet dungeon that is crawling with rats and smells like a pigsty." The words came in a rush, and now there was no stopping them. "Worst of all, sire, I bear the chain of iniquity and the heavy weight of guilt with me. I drag it with me every moment of every day. I sleep with it every night. I must be free of these shackles! I must be free! I cannot live unless I am free! I will try and try until I am free, or until I am dead! You will never—"

Josiah suddenly stopped, dismayed that he had dared say so much. He watched Argamor's face. The blacksmith's eyes narrowed and Josiah waited anxiously, afraid to even breathe.

Argamor abruptly turned on the two guards. "How did it happen?" he demanded.

"He cut his way out of his cell, my lord," Lawofsin explained. In spite of his own fear, Josiah noticed that the man's hands shook as he talked. "He made it through the gate leading to the inner ward, sire, and—"

"He what?" Enraged, Argamor took a threatening step forward, and his henchmen quickly stepped back. "Do mine ears deceive me? Did you say that this lad cut his way out of his cell?"

"Aye, that he did, my lord." Lawofsin was actually trembling now.

"How, pray tell? How could a scrawny lad like this cut his way out of his cell?" Argamor was pacing back and forth in his rage, clenching and unclenching his fists. His swarthy face was nearly purple, and the veins stood out in his neck. Josiah had never seen him so angry.

"The blame is not ours, my lord," Evilheart quickly assured

him. "It did not happen on our watch."

"Then whose watch was it, pray tell?" The furious blacksmith said the words slowly and distinctly, as though he was biting off the end of each word.

Evilheart hesitated. "It was—it was Heartless, my lord."

"I want him dead," Argamor growled. "This very day. Dispatch a message to the dungeon."

Josiah shuddered.

Argamor suddenly pointed a thick, dirty finger at Evilheart. "You did not tell me how it happened."

"He used a file, my lord." The guard nervously cleared his throat. "He cut through one of the bars in his cell."

"A file?"

"Aye, my lord. He took it from your workbench."

Argamor fell silent at this bit of information. He paced angrily back and forth behind the workbench, eyeing his two henchmen suspiciously. Evilheart and Lawofsin fidgeted apprehensively. Tension filled the shop.

"You said that he passed the inner gate."

"Aye, my lord."

"And just how did he accomplish that?"

"We don't know, my lord. We did find three keys on his person."

"Show me."

Lawofsin produced Father's Almsdeeds' golden keys and handed them to his master.

Argamor studied the keys for a moment. "Trifles. Worthless trifles." He turned and tossed them into the forge, and they melted away to nothing almost immediately. "Lad, where did you get these keys?"

Josiah did not want to implicate Father Almsdeeds, but he was afraid not to answer. "They were given to me, my lord, by a kind man named Father Almsdeeds."

"A man of the Church."

"Aye, my lord."

Argamor turned his attention back to Evilheart. "The lad did not open the gate with these trifles. But you have no idea how he did?"

"Nay, my lord."

Argamor scowled fiercely at Josiah. "How did you open the gate?"

"It—it opened by itself, sire. Or perhaps it was already open. I do not know."

To the boy's surprise, Argamor accepted his explanation. He turned back to Evilheart. "So he passed through the gate. Then what happened?"

"The lad couldn't climb the stairs due to the weight of guilt, my lord. We found him at the foot of the stairs."

"I see." Argamor was thoughtful for several long moments. Josiah stood trembling, waiting to see what would be the outcome of his attempt to escape from the Dungeon of Condemnation. He was exhausted, dreadfully so, but he stood stiffly, watching his master's face. Tension filled the shop like smoke from the forge.

Evilheart and Lawofsin stole quick, anxious glances at each other, and Josiah knew that they were as fearful as he was. Should Argamor think about the fact that the stolen file had been in his possession while they were on guard, they would also be implicated in his escape attempt. One guard had already been sentenced to die. In spite of their cruelty to him, Josiah actually felt sorry for them.

"Lad, the charges against you are very grievous," Argamor told Josiah, speaking slowly and deliberately as if to emphasize the importance of his words. "You have stolen tools from my shop, damaged dungeon property, and consorted with a man of the Church. But worst of all, you have attempted to escape from my domain." A dark look of intense hatred burned in the man's eyes. Josiah saw it and shuddered inwardly.

"I must not allow this to happen again. Ever again."

Josiah was terrified.

Argamor suddenly seized Josiah, lifted him from the floor, and placed him none too gently on his workbench. He grabbed the boy's leg and pulled it across the anvil. Snatching his hammer and a large chisel from the workbench, he turned and with lightning-quick movements struck several ringing blows. To Josiah's amazement, the chain of iniquity fell to the stone floor. He attempted to sit up, but a huge hand pushed him back down across the workbench.

Clank! Clank! A huge chain, nearly three times the size of the torturous one that he had worn so long, slammed down across the workbench just inches from his face. He heard the whoosh of the bellows and turned to see Argamor pumping with all his might. The forge glowed white-hot; smoke filled the room. Moments later the angry blacksmith turned toward Josiah with a glowing bar of metal held firmly in the tongs in his hand. Before the boy realized what was happening, Argamor had fused the heavy chain to the shackle on Josiah's ankle.

Josiah groaned inwardly. This new chain was huge; each link was nearly as wide as his hand! What a burden this would be to drag about wherever one went! But the worst was yet to come.

Argamor slammed a huge iron ingot on the workbench with an impact that seemed to shake the entire shop. He pumped the bellows again and smoke filled the room. The ringing blows of the hammer echoed in Josiah's ears. Within moments, the enormous weight was fastened to the huge chain on Josiah's ankle.

The cruel blacksmith dropped his hammer and tongs on the workbench. Placing a huge hand behind Josiah's head, he pulled the boy to a sitting position. "You shall never again worry about your old weight and chain," he said with an evil chuckle. "Behold, I have fashioned you new ones!" Seizing Josiah by the arms, he lifted him down from the workbench to stand upon the floor.

"Methinks the lad will not escape with these new fetters," he told Evilheart and Lawofsin, and all three men roared with laughter.

Josiah was aghast. "My lord, I can hardly move with this chain! I doubt if I can move this new weight of guilt! Have mercy, my lord, I beg you!"

But Argamor merely laughed. "I have never sought a reputation as a merciful man," he replied. His eyes narrowed. "But your work load shall not be diminished one iota, I assure you."

He placed the hammer on the anvil and returned the tongs to

Chapter Five

Evilheart and Lawofsin seemed to take delight in their preparations for Josiah's flogging. With broad smiles of amusement they dragged the terrified boy from the shop, pulled his tunic down around his waist to bare his thin shoulders and back, and then tied him to the sturdy trunk of the yew tree. Josiah's hands were pulled so tightly around the tree that it felt as if his arms would be torn from his shoulders.

"A coach approaches, my lord!" Evilheart announced in a voice that demanded attention.

"So let it come," Argamor retorted. "It is no concern to us."

"It's the royal coach, my lord," the guard lamented, "the Coach of Grace!"

"Ignore it. It will pass us by."

"My lord, the coach is turning into the yard! It is preparing to stop!" Josiah could sense the fear in the man's voice.

"What does he want here?" Argamor muttered.

Josiah strained to turn and see the coach that had his tormentors so worried, but he was bound to the yew tree so tightly that he could scarcely move. He heard the clatter of horses' their place in the tool rack on the wall. "We have remedied the problem; now for the punishment."

Josiah's heart sank at the words. Punishment? Would it not be punishment enough to drag this enormous chain and weight of guilt around all day? How much more could he bear?

"Tie him to the yew tree in the coal yard," he heard Argamor saying. "A severe flogging should drive all thoughts of escape from the heart of this rebellious slave."

"Somebody help me!" Josiah cried softly.

hooves, the creaking of the axletrees, the rumble of carriage wheels upon the hard earth. The snorting and breathing of the horses told him that the vehicle had come to a stop ten or fifteen paces from the tree.

"Argamor, release the lad!" The voice was powerful, weighted with an authority that demanded obedience. Somehow the voice reminded Josiah of the power of a rushing waterfall. He longed to turn and see the speaker, but could not.

"Your Majesty, the lad belongs to me," Argamor protested in a voice that was strangely submissive. "He has been rebellious, and we are merely chastening him for it."

"Release the lad," the voice commanded again. "Now."

"Aye, Your Majesty," Argamor replied. His voice was edged with fear and deference, and Josiah wondered who could command such respect from a man such as Argamor. "Lawofsin, release the lad." The blacksmith's voice trembled as he said the words, but Josiah could hear a trace of resentment.

Lawofsin stepped to the yew tree and untied Josiah's bonds. The boy turned around, pulling his tunic up around his shoulders as he did.

A gleaming white coach resplendent with golden fittings stood less than twenty paces from the tree. Above the majestic coach flew a royal purple standard emblazoned with the emblems of a cross and a golden crown; over the door were five lustrous letters: G-R-A-C-E. The boy stared hard at the letters, wishing he could read but somehow sensing that the word was one of glorious significance. Four snowy white horses stood proudly, impressive in their glittering gold harnesses. Josiah stared in amazement, completely overwhelmed by the grand sight. The magnificent vehicle was strangely out of place in the squalor and filth of the coal yard.

Behind the coach, a cavalcade of knights in shining armor sat astride snowy white chargers. The royal purple banner flying grandly from the tip of each man's lance carried the same cross and crown emblem as the coach. As Josiah watched, the knights dismounted and stood at attention beside their magnificent horses. The spirited chargers pranced and pawed the earth.

And then Josiah saw the King. A tall, commanding figure arrayed in an elegant scarlet robe, the King had his cloak open in the front, and Josiah could see a wide cummerbund of solid gold. The monarch was striding toward him, and his feet somehow had the appearance of polished brass. A glittering crown of pure gold rested upon his head. The King had hair like wool and eyes that burned like fire, and his countenance radiated love and concern. Josiah gazed in wonder at the King's face. Never before had he seen such a kind face. The King smiled at him, and his eyes were filled with love.

Josiah stole a glance at Argamor, and to his amazement, saw that the cruel blacksmith and his two henchmen were trembling. *Who is this King?* Josiah wondered in astonishment. *I wouldn't have known that Argamor was afraid of anyone!*

"I have come for the lad," the King said quietly. "I have purchased his freedom, and I have come to redeem him."

"Your Majesty, the lad is my slave forever," Argamor protested. "He is not for sale."

"That is not for you to decide, Argamor," the regal visitor replied sternly. "That is the lad's decision."

The King approached the awestruck boy. "Josiah, would you

be free of your chain?" The powerful voice was soft, gentle, soothing.

Trembling, Josiah stared up in astonishment at the King. "How do you know my name, sire?"

"I knew your name before I made the mountains," the King answered graciously. "Josiah, the choice is yours. Would you be free from your chain of iniquity, free from the weight of guilt, free from the abuse of your master, Argamor?"

Josiah's heart filled with longing, but fear and doubt gripped him. "Your Majesty, is that possible? How might I be free?"

The King smiled. "I have paid the price, Josiah, to purchase your freedom. Simply ask, lad, and you shall be set free."

Josiah stole another glance at Argamor. The burly blacksmith was glaring at him with an intense hatred that sent a bolt of fear through Josiah's being. A chill of terror swept over him, paralyzing him, rendering him helpless. He opened his mouth to speak, but under the malevolent eye of his abusive master, found that he could not. He longed to be free, but fear and doubt kept him rooted to the spot, unable to say a word.

The King reached out a gentle hand and touched him. "I am King Emmanuel, Lord of Creation, Lord of Eternity," he said, gazing deeply into Josiah's eyes. "All of Terrestria is my domain. Argamor has no claim on you. He cannot hurt you. Will you be free from his tyranny, and from your chain?"

Gazing fearfully into the gentle, loving eyes of King Emmanuel, Josiah suddenly found a deep settled peace. A gentle love radiated from the King, and he felt secure in its warmth. Finding himself drawn to the extraordinary ruler, he moved close to his side. "I must be free, Your Majesty. Please, set me free from my chain of iniquity, the weight of guilt, and from the cruel tyranny of Argamor. Please, my Lord."

"It is done," King Emmanuel said gently. Kneeling at Josiah's feet, the royal visitor reached down and grasped Josiah's chain in both hands. With one quick movement of his wrists, he twisted the sturdy iron link that fastened the chain of iniquity to Josiah's ankle, and the chain fell to the ground! The King then grasped the shackle around Josiah's ankle, twisted it, and shattered it into tiny fragments!

Josiah was in awe as he reached down to touch his ankle. "It is gone!" he cried in sheer delight. "It is really gone! I can hardly remember the time when I did not have a chain, and now it is gone!" Overcome with joy, he leaped high into the air. "I'm free! I'm free! My weight of guilt is gone!"

King Emmanuel smiled gently. "It is gone forever, my son. I have blotted out your sin and guilt, removed them from you as far as the east is from the west, placed them behind my back, and cast them into the depths of the sea. We shall remember them no more. Josiah, you have been justified!"

"Justified, Your Majesty?"

"Forgiven forever, Josiah. Your shackles are gone forever!"

At that moment, the leaden clouds overhead suddenly parted and a golden shaft of sunlight splashed across the coal yard, brilliant and dazzling to behold. The gleaming coach and the polished armor of the knights reflected the golden rays with such an intensity that Josiah had to turn away.

He stared at the ground where just moments before the huge chain of iniquity and the weight of guilt had lain. The torturous articles were nowhere to be seen.

Argamor stepped forward. "Your Majesty, I must protest—"

"Keep silent, Argamor," King Emmanuel ordered. "Josiah does not belong to you. I have redeemed him, and he belongs to me."

It was then that Josiah saw the terrible scar in the King's right hand. On the inside of Emmanuel's wrist was a fearsome wound, as if a large, sharp object had been driven into the King's flesh. As the kind ruler turned, the boy saw the same wound on the back of the King's hand, and he realized with great sadness that some sharp object had completely penetrated the hand. And then, to his dismay, he saw a similar wound in King Emmanuel's left hand. Not understanding the significance of what he was seeing, Josiah nevertheless realized that at one time or another King Emmanuel had been severely wounded. Pain racked his heart when he thought about it.

"This is yours, Josiah," King Emmanuel said, placing a shiny helmet on the boy's head. "It is the Helmet of Salvation. Wear it at all times. And this—" he reached inside his cloak and pulled out a roll of parchment—"is yours as well. It is your Assurance."

Josiah took the parchment from King Emmanuel's out-stretched hand, not yet understanding what it was. "I am grateful, Your Majesty."

King Emmanuel turned and called in the direction of the coach, "Truth! Mercy! Bring forth the best robe, and put it on Josiah! Put a ring on his hand, and shoes on his feet! Josiah was dead, and is alive again; he was lost, and is found."

At these words, two footmen dressed in royal blue livery hurried from the coach with the requested items. One of the servants carried a dazzling white robe shimmering with iridescent blue highlights, which he handed to King Emmanuel. "Hands over your head, Josiah," the King commanded. When the boy complied, the King slipped the exquisite garment over his head and pulled it into place. Josiah lowered his arms. "You are clothed in my Robe of Righteousness," Emmanuel announced.

Josiah's heart pounded with joy as he surveyed the shimmering new garment, so pure and white that it almost hurt one's eyes to look at it. "I thank you, Your Majesty," he said softly. The next item of clothing was a blue-and-black striped doublet with long sleeves, which he slipped on over the Robe of Righteousness. A sleeveless jerkin of soft, pale deerskin went over that and was tied closely around the waist. After donning a pair of trunk hose and a stunning, gold-and-blue patterned cloak, Josiah bore no resemblance to the struggling slave boy who had languished under Argamor's cruelty.

Pulling the gorgeous fabric of the robe away from his chest to examine it more closely, Josiah was amazed to find that his own dirty rags had vanished from beneath the new garments, and that he was spotlessly clean within. He stared at his hands in astonishment; even his fingernails were pink and clean. Not a trace of coal dust remained to remind him of his years of servitude to Argamor.

"This ring is the symbol of the Royal Family," King Emmanuel said, taking Josiah's hand and placing a glittering gold ring on his finger. "It is a token of your relationship to me." Josiah studied the ring. A huge sapphire gleamed with a brilliant blue light. In the center of the gem, the outline of a tiny shield was etched in gold; in the center of the shield, a tiny golden crown was superimposed over a tiny golden cross. Josiah was astounded to realize that the ring bore King Emmanuel's own coat of arms.

One of the footmen knelt and slipped new shoes onto Josiah's feet, and the boy found that they fit him perfectly. "Shoes for your feet," King Emmanuel stated, "so that you are fitted for service."

The King looked the boy over. "Every inch a prince," he announced grandly. He placed a strong, gentle hand on Josiah's shoulder. "Fear not:" he told Josiah, "for I have redeemed you, I have called you by your name; you are mine. You are precious in my sight, and I have loved you."

Tears of joy filled Josiah's eyes and he found himself throwing his arms around his new Master. His heart overflowed. It was wonderful to be forgiven, to be free, to be loved! "My Lord," Josiah said fervently, "I shall serve you forever!"

King Emmanuel's strong arms returned the embrace. "I am going away, Josiah, and you shall not see my face for a time. You are traveling to the Castle of Faith; I have made the arrangements. There you shall learn to serve me. Be faithful, Josiah. Watch for my return. And you must never forget: you are free from Argamor forever; he has no authority over you."

Truth opened the door of the regal coach and stood waiting. "Go quickly, Josiah," King Emmanuel urged. "You have much to learn, but you shall be a faithful servant of the cross. Mercy and Truth shall go with you, and the Coach of Grace shall carry you to the Castle of Faith."

"But when will I see you again?" Josiah asked, his heart filled with longing for the one who had set him free. "Will you not accompany me to the Castle of Faith?"

"I must go to the Golden City of the Redeemed and prepare a place for you," King Emmanuel replied, "but I will come again and receive you unto myself, that where I am, there you may be also."

"When will you come back?" Josiah begged.

"I cannot tell you, but it will not be long. Endure temptation; be faithful unto death, and I will give you a crown of life. Josiah, you are mine. I have loved you with an everlasting love: therefore with lovingkindness have I drawn you. My father has loved you with the very same love."

Josiah walked slowly toward the coach with his heart overflowing with love for the wondrous King who had redeemed him and set him free. Remembering that the heavy chain of iniquity and weight of guilt had been removed, he leaped high in the air for joy. At the rear of the coach, the cavalcade of knights mounted their splendid chargers and prepared to ride.

Carrying the precious parchment, Josiah stepped into the coach and timidly took a seat upon a cushion of scarlet velvet at the rear of the coach. The door closed, and the coach started forward. Seated directly across from Josiah was an elderly man with a long, white beard. The stranger was dressed in a stunning green doublet trimmed in gold braid. A black cloak patterned with gold thread hung loosely about his shoulders. Perched on the back of the seat behind the old man was a snowy white dove of unusual beauty.

"Welcome, Prince Josiah," the old man greeted him warmly, smiling and showing a set of beautiful white teeth in the midst of his beard. "Welcome to the Royal Family."

Josiah felt himself immediately drawn to the old man. "I thank you, sire. I don't know who you were expecting, but I am not Prince Josiah." He gave a nervous laugh. "Up until a few moments ago, I was just a lowly slave. Your King just set me free."

The white-haired old man merely smiled. "Oh, but you are a prince. You are Prince Josiah, royal heir with King Emmanuel."

Josiah laughed. "You must have me confused with someone else, kind sire. Of a truth, my name is Josiah, but I am not a prince. I am just a common slave."

The man's smile broadened. "Apparently you do not fully understand what has happened to you today," he said kindly, "but I am prepared to explain it to you more fully." He held out a slender hand. "My prince, might I see your parchment, please?"

Josiah held back, unwilling to part with the precious parchment. "Who are you, sire?"

"I am Sir Faithful, steward of the Castle of Faith. King Emmanuel has entrusted me with the keeping of the castle until his return. I serve with Lord Watchful, the castle's constable, or castellan, who is charged with the castle's protection." He held out his hand again. "May I?"

Josiah studied his elderly companion. The old steward's eyes glowed with a peace and joy that gave silent testimony to the fact that he was indeed a servant to King Emmanuel. Josiah handed the parchment to him.

Sir Faithful carefully unrolled the parchment, and Josiah saw that the page was filled with a bold, flowing script and stamped at the bottom with an official-looking seal. The document was impressive, but the words meant nothing to Josiah. "What does it say, sire?" he begged.

"'Be it known to all men everywhere,'" the old man read aloud, "'that from this day henceforth and forever, Josiah Everyman, of the Village of Despair, has been adopted into the

Royal Family of King Emmanuel and shall henceforth be known as Prince Josiah, heir eternal with King Emmanuel.' It's signed and sealed with His Majesty's own seal, Your Highness, making it official and forever unrevokeable. You are a prince, lad. Prince Josiah."

"But—but are you certain, sire? How can that be?"

Sir Faithful laughed and pointed to the parchment. "It is written in His Majesty's own hand, Prince Josiah."

Josiah was awestruck. "I—I didn't know," he stammered. He leaned out the coach window, and, turning to the rear, watched Argamor's loathsome shop recede in the distance, growing smaller and smaller and smaller until it was merely a speck on the horizon. "From a slave to a prince in just one day," he said in awe. "How could such a thing be?"

"It's called 'grace'," Sir Faithful said quietly.

Chapter Six

The Coach of Grace rolled swiftly down the driveway and turned into the lane with the cavalcade of knights riding smartly along behind. Josiah sank back into the luxurious seats and sighed with contentment. "I enjoyed the Inn of Provision, Sir Faithful. Never in my life have I eaten so much in one meal! I had more food today than I usually get in a month!"

The old steward laughed pleasantly. "King Emmanuel provides for his own. From this day forward you will dine at His Majesty's own table and eat of his bounty." He eyed Prince Josiah's slender frame. "From the looks of things, I'd say that you can use it."

He smiled. "From this day forward, my prince, your life will be completely different. Argamor had nothing but hatred and contempt for you; King Emmanuel has nothing but love and concern. Argamor searched for ways to make your life miserable; His Majesty will do everything to make your life one of joy and fulfillment. With Argamor as your master, you faced nothing but a life of futility and despair; with Emmanuel as your Lord, your future holds delights of the soul such as you cannot not possibly imagine. And when someday you are called to the Golden City, you will know joy and contentment beyond measure."

The coach rolled along smoothly, although the road was rutted and rough. Josiah fell silent. Sir Faithful watched him for several moments. "What is on your mind, Prince Josiah? The eyes are the windows of a man's soul, and your eyes reveal that your thoughts are troubled. Tell me, my prince, what troubles you so?"

"Am I really free of Lord Argamor?" Josiah asked slowly. "I've been his slave for as long as I can remember. What if—" He fell silent, unwilling to continue, as if the act of verbalizing his fearful thoughts would bring them to pass.

Sir Faithful looked at him questioningly. "Please continue, my prince."

Josiah took a deep breath. "How do I know that Lord Argamor can't come sometime and demand that I go back to his foul blacksmith shop and work for him again? How do I know that I am really free forever? How do I know that I am a prince? I certainly don't feel like one. I just feel like Josiah—Josiah the slave."

"First of all, Prince Josiah, you must never again refer to that cruel taskmaster as 'Lord' Argamor. No longer is he your master, nor your lord. His power over you is broken forever."

Josiah nodded silently. Reassured, his heart thrilled at the words.

"How do you know that you are really free forever?" the old man continued, and a soft light seemed to flicker in his eyes. "How do you know that you are a prince? You have King Emmanuel's word on it, Prince Josiah."

"But I don't feel like a prince. How do I know that Lord Arg—that Argamor can't come and make me work for him, or take me back to the Dungeon of Condemnation?"

"Your salvation is not based upon your feelings, lad," Sir Faithful said quietly.

"Salvation?" The word was new to Josiah.

"It means being set free from your chain of iniquity and weight of guilt," the old man explained. "It means being saved from Argamor, and from the Dungeon of Condemnation. It means being adopted into the Royal Family. Salvation is what took place today."

"Oh." Josiah was thoughtful. "Salvation. I like the word."

"Tis a grand word, indeed," Sir Faithful agreed. "But as I was saying, your salvation is not dependent upon your feelings." He held up the parchment. "Your salvation, and your new position as Prince Josiah, is dependent upon the word of His Majesty. His own royal seal is upon the document." He unrolled the parchment. "Shall I read it again?"

Josiah nodded. "Please do."

When Sir Faithful had finished reading and had re-rolled the parchment, Josiah nodded happily. "It does say that, doesn't it? And it's in the King's own handwriting."

The old steward nodded in agreement. "Aye, that it does, lad, that it does."

A songbird flew in through the window of the coach just then, landed upon the sill, and sang a song of praise. Josiah and the old man listened in silence. When the song was finished, the little bird flitted back through the window and was gone.

"I saw a terrible wound in King Emmanuel's hand," Josiah said thoughtfully. "In fact, he had wounds in both hands."

"There are similar wounds in His Majesty's feet as well," Sir Faithful told him.

Josiah looked at him in alarm. "What happened, sire?"

"Did you hear what His Majesty told Argamor? 'I have purchased his freedom, and I have come to redeem him.' The wounds in your King's hands are the marks of his great love for you, Prince Josiah. He received those wounds when he purchased your soul and your freedom."

Josiah was shocked. "But how, sire? How did it happen?"

"It didn't just happen, my prince. Your redemption was planned before the foundation of Terrestria."

"Sire, tell me about it," Josiah begged.

"There's a special place outside the City of Zion," Sir Faithful began. "It's the place of redemption, the place where your salvation was purchased. King Emmanuel went to that place and gave his blood so that you might be forgiven and set free. He died in your place, taking the penalty for your chain of iniquity and weight of guilt."

"But why would he die for me?"

"He loved you, Prince Josiah."

"And that's why he could set me free today," Josiah whispered softly.

"Exactly."

Josiah was puzzled as he turned and faced the steward. "But if King Emmanuel died for me, how did he come back to life?"

"King Emmanuel is not an ordinary man, Prince Josiah. He died for you outside the City of Zion, and then came back to life three days later."

Josiah frowned. "That's astounding!"

Sir Faithful nodded. "Indeed it is, lad."

"How did he die?"

"He was executed, Prince Josiah, and he willingly died in your place. He died the most painful death you can imagine." Sir Faithful quietly told the story of King Emmanuel's death, and by the time he had finished, the young prince was in tears.

They rode in silence for a time. Josiah thought about King Emmanuel and the great sacrifice that the King had made to set him free, and his heart swelled with even greater love for his new Master. *It's hard to believe that anyone could love me so,* he thought gratefully. *King Emmanuel, you have my loyalty forever!*

Josiah stuck his head out the coach window and watched the passing scenery. The countryside seemed so beautiful with its wooded hills, winding streams, and bright meadows. The hillsides were alive with the colors of autumn, and Josiah took a deep breath of the fragrant air. *I know the one who made all this,* he thought grandly. *I am actually part of his family!*

The coach rolled through a busy little village and the townspeople stopped in their scurrying here and there to watch the majestic coach with its escort of stately knights. Josiah watched the faces of the peasants as they lined the narrow street, staring in fascinated awe at the regal vehicle. Some wore expressions of sheer delight as they waved at the passing coach; others stared silently with rigid limbs and somber faces. In one open-sided shanty, Josiah saw a blacksmith pause at his anvil to watch the coach pass and he thought immediately of Argamor. *How splendid it is to be free of that hateful place,* he thought gratefully.

As the Coach of Grace left the little village behind, Josiah thought again of Father Almsdeeds. *I wonder why his golden keys could not free me from the Dungeon of Condemnation. He seemed so eager to help. And yet, the three keys he gave me did absolutely nothing.* He looked up to find Sir Faithful watching him closely.

"What are you thinking, my prince?" the old steward asked gently. "Your thoughts are troubled again."

"When I was in the Dungeon of Condemnation, a man of the Church gave me three keys to set me free," Josiah answered slowly, thoughtfully. "His name was Father Almsdeeds, and he seemed like a really helpful man. But when I tried the keys he gave me, they did absolutely nothing. They didn't set me free— they didn't do anything at all!"

"Describe the keys," Sir Faithful requested.

"They were golden, set with precious jewels, and very beautiful to behold," the young prince replied. "They had words on them that I could not read, but Father Almsdeeds told me they were the Keys of Religion, Penance, and Sincerity. Each of them fit quite nicely into the lock, but when I turned each key, it did nothing! The door was still locked!"

"My prince, did you not wonder how Father Almsdeeds got into the Dungeon of Condemnation to give you the keys?" Sir Faithful asked.

"What do you mean, sire?"

"Father Almsdeeds was a prisoner in the Dungeon of Condemnation with you. He has a chain of his own, though perhaps you did not notice it. His keys are worthless, Prince Josiah, or he would have used them to set himself free. Argamor allows him to wander the inner ward, giving false hope to other sufferers like him. But his golden keys, beautiful as they are, can never set a man free. Only King Emmanuel can do that. If the Keys of Religion, Penance or Sincerity could set a prisoner free, His Majesty would not have died in your place."

Late that afternoon, Sir Faithful looked out the window and announced, "We're almost there. The Castle of Faith is just ahead."

Josiah stuck his head out the coach window. The Coach of Grace was rolling through a pleasant little village. The towns-people looked happy as they hurried along the tidy streets; the shops and houses were neat and well kept.

Three or four furlongs away, a majestic castle of white stone glistened in the afternoon sun. Situated high atop a rocky pali-sade that jutted out into a sapphire-blue sea, the Castle of Faith rose majestically above the surrounding countryside. With its high walls and many towers, the castle was an imposing edifice, visible from many furlongs away. Josiah counted four round tow-ers rising above the front wall, one at each corner and two in the middle, and he could see similar towers toward the rear of the castle. The familiar royal purple standard with the cross and crown flew grandly from the top of each tower. A winding road climbed the steep castle approach to cross a sturdy drawbridge leading to the massive front gate at the northwest corner. Below the bridge, a water-filled moat abutted the wall. The Castle of Faith was protected on three sides by the sea and on the north side by the moat.

The Coach of Grace rolled up the steep lane toward the front gate. Chains rattled as the portcullis, a massive, ironclad grat-ing, rose slowly to allow them entrance. Behind the portcullis, immense oaken gates parted in the middle and swung open to admit the royal coach. Three trumpeters on the battlements above the gatehouse sounded a welcome.

Josiah was impressed by the security of the high walls and massive gates. "No one could ever get into the Castle of Faith unless he was invited, could he?"

"We must never take that for granted, my prince," Sir Faithful replied quietly. "Captain Diligence and Captain Assurance work day and night to prevent that very occurrence, but we must all be alert and watchful."

The Coach of Grace rolled to a stop and the door opened. Truth stood stiffly at attention as he held the door for the coach's passengers to alight. Sir Faithful rose to his feet. "Welcome to the Castle of Faith, Prince Josiah," he said grandly. "Welcome home."

Josiah descended the steps to find himself within a narrow courtyard surrounded by the towering castle walls. "This is the west barbican," Sir Faithful told him. "It's like an extension of the gatehouse. When we pass through that gate to the left, we'll be in the castle proper."

Josiah's heart pounded with anticipation as he followed his guide through the massive second gate and entered the corridor. Two companies of knights in shining armor, one on each side of the passageway, stood stiffly at attention. Beyond the soldiers, a throng of nearly a hundred people lined the approach to a large courtyard. They cheered at the sight of the new prince.

"This is the main bailey, or courtyard," Sir Faithful whispered, as a tall man in a bright green jerkin and brown leggings approached. "The knights before you are the two garrisons under

57

the commands of Captain Diligence and Captain Assurance. The people assembled in the bailey are the castle's residents. They're known as the 'Ecclesia', or 'called-out ones'. You shall meet many of them later. The man approaching us now is Lord Watchful, the castle constable, and he's the one responsible for the security of the Castle of Faith while King Emmanuel is away. I serve with him."

A golden sword swung at Lord Watchful's side as he strode briskly across the cobblestones and greeted Josiah warmly. "Welcome, Prince Josiah, to the Castle of Faith! I am Lord Watchful, at your service. And how was your journey?"

"It was magnificent," Josiah replied. "I am delighted to be here, Lord Watchful, and delighted to be free!"

"We are delighted to have you here," the constable replied. "Supper will be served within the hour." He turned to Sir Faithful. "Why not take him up to his solar, sire, and let him get settled in?"

Josiah followed Sir Faithful across the bailey, through a narrow doorway, and up three flights of stairs. They came out into the open on a narrow walkway that ran along the top of the castle wall. Josiah leaned over the battlements and looked down upon the Coach of Grace parked in the west barbican. "We're up mighty high, aren't we?"

Sir Faithful laughed. "As you can see, the Castle of Faith is a concentric castle, meaning that there are two rings of protective stone walls. The inner wall is higher than the outer so that our castle defenders can fire at the enemy over the lower outer walls. The walls are called 'curtains', and they are six yards thick at the bottom."

BOOK ONE: THE TERRESTRIA CHRONICLES

Beyond the outer walls of the castle Josiah saw the small town through which the coach had passed. From his vantage atop the battlements he could see the villagers as they hurried on various errands through the narrow, perfectly straight streets. They looked happy; their faces bore expressions of peace and contentment. "What village is this I see?" Josiah asked.

"That is the Village of Dedication," Sir Faithful replied. "The townspeople are all loyal servants to King Emmanuel, and they depend upon the Castle of Faith for protection in times of danger or distress."

He led the way along the narrow walkway. "This is called the 'sentry walk.' "

Josiah ran his hand along the rough stone of the castle wall as they walked. "Why are there gaps in the battlement?" he asked. "The top of the castle wall, ah, curtain, looks like it has teeth."

"Those gaps are called 'crenels', and they allow archers to shoot through. The raised parts between the crenels are called the 'merlons', and the archers can take cover behind them."

They followed the sentry walk to a door in the northhwest tower, and Sir Faithful opened it. "Prince Josiah, this will be your solar."

Josiah was puzzled. "Solar?"

"Your quarters," the steward explained. "This is where you will stay." Josiah stepped into a round room with a fireplace on one side and a narrow window on the other. Fragrant reeds covered the wooden floor. Colorful tapestries graced the stone walls between the fireplace and the window. Beneath a large tapestry of a lion was a huge, soft bed. Nearby stood a bench and a chiffonnier with three drawers. A washbasin and ewer sat on a small wooden stand beneath the window. To the right of the fireplace, a narrow, winding staircase disappeared through an opening in the ceiling.

Glancing up at the stairs, Josiah was surprised to see a dove just like the one that he had seen in the Coach of Grace. The beautiful white bird was perched on the top stair, looking down at him with dark, unblinking eyes.

Josiah sat on the edge of the bed, marveling at the way his body sank into the soft mattress. "Is this where I am to sleep, sire? I am unaccustomed to such finery."

The steward laughed. "It is pleasant, is it not? King Emmanuel prepared it for you."

After a moment Josiah stood to his feet and gazed about the room. His face took on a somber, thoughtful look, and Sir Faithful noticed. "You are thinking of your cell in the Dungeon of Condemnation, are you not?"

Josiah nodded. "Aye. When I left my cold, dark cell this morning, I never dreamed that I would never have to occupy it again. I hated that place! It was so dark, so cold, so... so dreary and lonely. I am thankful to be here."

He stepped to the narrow window and looked out at the sea. Far below, golden sunlight shimmered on the surface of the water. "What have I done, Sir Faithful, to deserve all this?"

The steward slipped over beside the young prince and put a gentle hand on his shoulder. "Nothing, Prince Josiah, absolutely nothing. This was provided for you simply because King Emmanuel loved you. Take my advice, lad, and be careful to always remember what our gracious King has done for you."

"Oh, I will never forget, sire," Josiah said easily. "I am grateful, forever grateful, for the grace that King Emmanuel has bestowed upon me. I can never forget."

"Don't say that so hastily," Sir Faithful warned. "Today your heart is full of wonder and awe at the grace of King Emmanuel and what he has done for you, but how easily that is lost. If you lose the wonder of your salvation, your heart can quickly become cold, and the enemy will have the advantage over you. Be careful; guard your heart for your King."

At that moment, footsteps sounded on the sentry walk outside, and there came a sudden knock on the door.

Chapter Seven

Josiah and Sir Faithful turned at the sound of the knock at the door. The steward opened it to find a slender youth standing on the sentry walk. "Begging your pardon, Sir Faithful," the boy said, bowing low, "but supper is served in ten minutes."

"I thank you, Mathias," the steward replied. The boy bowed again and hurried away.

The prince and the steward stepped out onto the sentry walk and closed the solar door behind them. The sun was disappearing behind the forest to the west, and as the purple twilight and blue shadows descended over the land, the castle walls turned golden with the refracted light. Sir Faithful paused with his hand upon the door latch. "Let's go up on the roof of the tower for just a moment. This is my favorite time of the day."

Josiah followed him back into the solar, up the narrow stairs by the fireplace, and out onto a narrow sentry walk on the roof of the tower. The Castle of Faith lay below them, glowing pink and amber in the rays from the dying sun. "You can see the entire castle from here," the old man told Josiah.

"That's the great hall to the right," he said, pointing to a large structure against the south wall of the bailey. "That's where the castle meals are served, and that's where King Emmanuel holds court when he is in attendance at the castle. The kitchens are right across the bailey from the great hall."

He leaned over the tower battlements. "The tower farthest from us, on the southeast corner, is the King's tower. His solar is just this side of it. See the archways across the east end of the bailey? They lead to the east bailey, which is another courtyard identical to the one directly below us. The stables, blacksmith shop, and armory are all located at the end of the east bailey. I know the castle is a bit confusing at first, with all the different levels, doors, towers and passageways, but you will soon learn your way around."

He turned toward the stairs. "Let's head down to the great hall, shall we? We don't want to miss supper at the King's table!"

Moments later Josiah and Sir Faithful entered an immense, open room with a high, expansive ceiling supported by massive beams. At one end of the great hall, a huge hearth blazed brightly with a warm fire. Immense wrought iron chandeliers ablaze with numerous candles hung over the hall from heavy chains. Three rows of long trestle tables flanked by benches occupied the center of the room. A long table at right angles to the others enjoyed a place of prominence in front of the huge fireplace. The table was ornate, set with silver service, and flanked by upholstered chairs in place of benches. Josiah guessed immediately that it was King Emmanuel's table.

Knights and their ladies were strolling casually into the great hall, laughing and conversing warmly with each other. Squires and pages called to each other, and children laughed and chattered happily. Ladies-in-waiting exchanged greetings with members of the castle staff while servants and scullions hurried here and there, filling goblets and bearing platters of food. A minstrel stood in one corner, frowning in concentration as he tuned the strings on his lute. In the noisy hustle and bustle of the preparation for the evening meal, the atmosphere in the great hall was one of anticipation, happiness and contentment.

Attendants and pages stood at attention along the walls, and above their heads, the high stone walls of the great hall were adorned with brightly-colored vertical banners of silk and satin. The banners had various emblems embroidered into the fabric, each banner unique and different from its neighbors. Josiah gazed in fascination at the colorful banners.

Sir Faithful noticed his interest. "The banners are taken from the constellations," he explained. "Each banner is a reminder of King Emmanuel, and depicts an aspect of his royal character."

Josiah was puzzled. "I don't understand."

"See the banner with the loaf of bread? King Emmanuel is the Bread of Life; we can't live without him. The banner with the lantern reminds us that he is the Light of Terrestria, and guides us on our path in life."

Josiah pointed to a banner with the image of a shepherd. "So that one means that His Majesty is also a Shepherd, who takes care of us?"

Sir Faithful nodded. "Aye, that's exactly right."

"What about that one, the one with the door on it? What does that mean? And what is that one, with the flower on it?"

"That flower is the lily of the valley. Think about them for a while."

The prince and the steward made their way to the King's

table. Lord Watchful, Captain Assurance, Captain Diligence, and their ladies joined them at the table. An attendant rang a silver bell, and the castle's residents quickly took their places around their respective tables. A hush fell across the great hall.

Lord Watchful stood to his feet. "We wish to honor our King and show our gratitude for his provision," he announced. The constable held a rolled parchment in his right hand. He opened his hand, and to Josiah's astonishment, the parchment vanished.

Moments later, attendants swarmed around the tables, bearing platters and chargers and large bowls of food. The great hall was filled with tantalizing aromas. Josiah sat back and watched in amazement. This was more food than he had ever seen in his entire life!

An attendant appeared at his left elbow. "At your service, Your Highness." He handed Josiah a small platter with a large, flat piece of brown bread upon it.

"I thank you," Josiah said politely, disappointed that he was being served bread when there were so many different foods to choose from. He placed the platter in front of him and picked up the slice of bread, preparing to take a bite.

Sir Faithful noticed. "Prince Josiah," he whispered, "don't eat that bread. It is your trencher. Place your food upon the bread. It will absorb the juices."

A regular procession of attendants filed by, bearing platters of miniature meat pastries, pheasant in cinnamon sauce, beef fritters, eels in spicy puree, loaches in cold green sauce, slices of roast mutton, filets of saltwater fish, and various garden vegetables. Josiah took some of each, completely filling his platter. "I've never seen so much food!" he whispered to Sir Faithful.

The steward smiled. "You are at His Majesty's table," he whispered back.

Josiah reached in with both hands and began to eat, enjoying the rich and unusual delicacies of the royal feast. The flaky pastries filled with tender venison, the hot, spicy fritters, the steaming vegetables smothered in butter, the succulent slices of mutton—it was indeed a feast fit for a king, and Josiah was enjoying every morsel. The minstrel strolled among the tables, strumming his lute and singing ballads that told of the greatness of King Emmanuel.

One song in particular caught Josiah's attention:

"I sing the greatness of my King, my Lord Emmanuel
His power is great and far exceeds
What mortal tongue or pen can tell.
My heart is full; I sing for him,
And trust that I may serve him well.

I sing the love of my great King, my Lord Emmanuel
His lovingkindness ransomed me,
But why he did, I cannot tell.
His love led him to die for me.
I trust that I may serve him well."

The song went on to tell of the horrible dungeon of sin in which the minstrel had once been imprisoned, the pain and agony of servitude to sin, and how the gracious hand of King Emmanuel had reached down and set him free. Listening to the story presented in song, Josiah found his own eyes filled with tears. *That's exactly what happened to me!* His heart throbbed with love and adoration for his King.

Josiah reverently touched the golden ring upon his hand,

using his fingertip to trace the design of the King's coat of arms in the center of the magnificent sapphire. He sat back with a sigh of contentment, thoroughly enjoying the warmth of the crackling fire upon the hearth, the exquisite food, the cheerful, loving companionship of those about him, and the beautiful music praising his King. His soul was at peace.

By the time he had emptied his platter his hunger had vanished. Just then, another procession of attendants filed in. The steaming platters bore roast lamb, cuts of freshwater fish, bacon with broth, veal basted in almond sauce, chicken pasties and crisps, and bream pasties. Josiah stared. "Sire, where did all this food come from?" he whispered to Sir Faithful. "We already have enough."

"This is just the second course," the steward explained.

"The second course, sire?"

"There's a third course to follow," Sir Faithful said with an amused twinkle in his eye, "followed, of course, by the sweets and confections."

Josiah filled his plate with various items from the second course, being careful to take smaller portions. An attendant appeared at his elbow with a huge silver platter. In the center was the figure of a lion sculpted from fruit jelly. "Would you care for some, Your Highness?"

By the time the feast was over, Josiah felt as if he would never need to eat again. As he wiped his hands on a stiff linen napkin, his eyes filled with tears. "I had half a bowl of cold barley gruel this morning," he whispered to Sir Faithful. "That's all that Argamor ever gave me—just enough to keep me alive. But now, sire, look at the feast that King Emmanuel has provided for me!"

"Aye," the steward agreed. "King Emmanuel is a better master by far, is he not?"

Josiah was thoughtful as he climbed the stairs to his solar that night, carrying a lamp to light his way. *King Emmanuel has been so good to me and I really haven't done anything to deserve it! Setting me free from the chain of iniquity and the weight of guilt*—he reached down and felt his ankle as if to reassure himself that it was really true—*bringing me here to the Castle of Faith, making me a prince, even though I don't feel like one!* He reached the sentry walk just then. Overwhelmed by the events of the day, he paused and looked up at the starry sky. "I thank you, my King," he whispered softly. "I know you cannot hear me, but I am grateful. I will serve you the rest of my life!"

As he gazed in silence at a group of stars glittering against a backdrop of dark velvet directly overhead, he slowly realized that together they formed the image of a man—a shepherd holding a staff, just as he had seen on the banner in the great hall. "Emmanuel," he breathed in awe. "Emmanuel, the great shepherd. The image of my new Lord is in the heavens above me. I wonder why I never saw that before."

Fascinated, he studied the starry heavens for several moments, overwhelmed with wonder as he began to recognize the various constellations. To the north he found a group of stars that very clearly formed the shape of a lantern, and to the south, a glittering cluster that depicted a loaf of bread. In the east, the twinkling stars formed a beautiful image that he recognized as a lily of the valley. Enthralled, the young prince scanned the starry skies for several long moments, trying to find the other constellations that he knew depicted the various aspects of Emmanuel's character, but could find no others. With a long sigh of contentment and wonder, he turned toward his solar. The witness of the glittering celestial bodies above the castle created within him a deep sense of satisfaction—his new master was not only Lord of all Terrestria, but also of the vast heavens above him.

Just then the sentry passed him on the top of the battlement. "Good night, Prince Josiah."

Startled, Josiah looked up. "Good night, sire."

Reaching his solar, he opened the door and slipped inside, then set the lamp on the stand with the washbasin. *What an unforgettable day this has been,* he told himself as he slipped out of his new clothes. *I got up this morning as a slave in a dungeon, and I'm going to bed tonight as a prince in a castle! I am now the son of the Lord of all Terrestria!* He slipped into the bed and then leaned over and blew out the lamp. *I just hope I don't wake up in the morning to find out that it's all just a dream.*

Josiah awakened the next morning to find sunlight streaming in through the narrow window. He lay still for a moment, staring at the unfamiliar surroundings, trying to figure out where he was. Suddenly it all came back. *I am a prince! I am no longer the slave of Argamor! The chain of iniquity and the weight of guilt are gone forever!* Cautiously, almost fearfully, he drew back the bedclothes until he could see his ankle. It was true after all—the dreadful shackle was gone forever. He jumped out of bed and leaped to the window to gaze down at the azure blue sea below. "What a glorious day!"

He dressed hurriedly. Just as he finished, he heard a gentle knock at the door. He opened it to find a twisted, bent little man standing on the sentry walk. The little man bowed low. "Your Highness, I am Sir Preparation. I have come to outfit you with armor. If you are ready, there is time to equip you before breakfast."

Josiah was surprised. "I just got here yesterday evening!"

Sir Preparation nodded. "But it is wise to be prepared as soon as possible, my prince. Remember, we are in a war."

A nearby door opened just then, and Sir Faithful appeared. "Good morning, Prince Josiah," he said. "I see you have met Sir Preparation, the Castle of Faith's chief armorer."

Josiah and Sir Faithful followed Sir Preparation along the sentry walk on the south side. The little man walked with a strange, hopping gait, causing his head to bob up and down with each step. Josiah watched him, amused by the spectacle. Sir Faithful noticed. "Any man may serve King Emmanuel," he whispered sternly, "not just the tall and the strong. This man is one of the best armorers in all Terrestria."

Reproved, Josiah nodded meekly.

The trio took four flights of stairs down to the armory, which was located in the basement beside the southeast tower. "I believe I have everything in your size," the armorer told Josiah, "but if not, I can readily make what you require." As Josiah entered the armory, his eyes were drawn to the glowing forge along one wall. Helmets, weapons, and various pieces of armor lined the other three stone walls.

"You already have your salet, or Helmet of Salvation," the little man said, looking over his display of assorted pieces of armor. "That is good." He selected a shiny piece of armor and turned toward Josiah. "Here—try this. It is the Breastplate of

Righteousness. It will protect your heart from the weapons of the wicked one." Sir Preparation held the breastplate against Josiah's chest, looked it over, and then strapped it into place. "A perfect fit!"

He selected a wide belt and handed it to the young prince. "I know this will fit. Gird your loins with Truth." Josiah fastened the Belt of Truth around his waist.

"Be seated, please, Prince Josiah." Kneeling on the floor, Sir Preparation selected two sabotons, steel shoes with sharp spiked toes. The armorer slipped a saboton on Josiah's left foot, and then one on his right. "Your feet," he announced, "are shod with the Preparation of the Gospel of Peace."

He stood to his feet and selected a shield from a huge assortment high on the wall. As he turned, Josiah saw the coat of arms emblazoned on the front of the shield: a cross and crown, like King Emmanuel's coat of arms, but with a second crown below it. "This is the most important of all," the armorer said, "the Shield of Faith, wherewith you shall be able to quench all the fiery darts of the wicked." He held it up, and Josiah slipped his left arm through the straps on the back.

"The coat of arms on the shield is similar to King Emmanuel's," Josiah said, "but with an additional crown. Pray tell, sire, what is the significance?"

"One day you shall reign with King Emmanuel. The second crown is a symbol of the rewards that lie ahead for you."

Josiah held the shield in front of his chest and stepped over in front of a full-length looking glass to see his reflection. "All I need now is a sword."

"The Sword of the Spirit," Sir Preparation agreed. "And here

71

it is." With these words, he handed Josiah a thick book bound in black leather.

Josiah frowned. "Sire, I cannot read."

"We shall start your lessons today."

"I need a sword," the boy protested, "not a book!"

"This is the finest sword ever made," Sir Preparation declared, taking the book from Josiah's hand. "When you know how to use it, you can defeat any foe!" Raising the book and holding it to one side, he slashed through the air with it. In an instant, the black book became a glittering sword, and the sharp point of the blade passed within inches of Josiah's face.

Josiah leaped backwards in alarm, and the armorer laughed. "There is no finer sword than this, my prince. Learn to use it and use it well, and no enemy shall be able to stand before you."

He handed Josiah the sword, and it became a little book again. Josiah swung the little book as he had seen Sir Preparation do and the book became a sharp sword. "Hold it to your side, and it becomes a book again," Sir Preparation instructed, "and then you can stow it within your doublet."

Josiah looked from one man to the other. "Why am I being equipped for battle? We are not in a war."

"Oh, but we are, Prince Josiah!" Sir Faithful answered swiftly. "The Castle of Faith may be attacked at any time. When you became a prince yesterday, you entered into that war with us. Our enemy is now your enemy."

"So who is this enemy?" Josiah inquired casually. "The Castle of Faith would keep him out, would it not?"

"Our enemy," both men replied in unison, "is Argamor!"

BOOK ONE: THE TERRESTRIA CHRONICLES

"Argamor?" Josiah echoed, with some confusion. "The mean-tempered blacksmith who spends his days forging chains and shackles of slavery?"

"Aye, the very same," Sir Faithful told him. "But he is more than just the mean-tempered blacksmith who forges chains. Argamor is actually a powerful warlord. He's known as the Prince of this World, Lord of the Realm of Darkness. In the ancient language, his name is Apollyon, which means 'Destroyer'. He is the sworn enemy of King Emmanuel, and he is determined to take the Castle of Faith and everyone in it."

Josiah took an experimental swing with the sword. "But why, Sir Faithful? What does he want with the Castle of Faith?"

"Many, many years ago, Argamor was actually the servant of King Emmanuel," the elderly steward explained, stroking his beard as he talked. "This was in the First Age of Terrestria, long before the Great Battle of the Kings. Argamor was the chief musician for His Majesty, I believe, and served faithfully in the Golden City, the City of the Redeemed. But after a time he decided to try to usurp King Emmanuel's throne."

"And become the king of Terrestria?" Josiah asked.

"Aye, lad," Sir Faithful responded. "And when he revolted against King Emmanuel, he took one-third of His Majesty's army with him!"

"Sire, how did he do that?"

"Those troops decided that Argamor would win and they sided with him, I suppose. They joined in the revolt and fought against the King. There was a fierce battle in the Golden City, which we now refer to as the First Great War, and Argamor's forces were defeated. King Emmanuel banished

Argamor and his followers from the Golden City and there has been war ever since."

"That's why the Castle of Faith was built," the little armorer added, "to protect this region of Terrestria against an attack by Argamor and his forces."

Josiah was amazed. "I had no idea," he said slowly. "I always thought that Argamor was just a blacksmith! He was brutal. He was vicious. He was a cruel slave master, and I knew that we were making chains to enslave other poor souls, but I had no idea who Argamor really was!"

"All of Terrestria is divided," Sir Faithful went on. "Some are loyal to King Emmanuel, while others have sided with Argamor. There are those who think that they've not chosen sides, but no one is neutral. You are either for His Majesty, or for Argamor. Those who have rejected King Emmanuel have chosen to side with Argamor, whether they realize it or not."

Prince Josiah took another mighty swing with the sword. "I'm beginning to understand why we have the castle, and why I need the armor. I had no idea that a war was coming."

"The Great War has been raging for centuries," the elderly steward told him, "but it is going to get worse. There's a fierce battle coming soon that will make everyone in Terrestria decide once and for all which side they are on. We need to be ready."

Chapter Eight

Josiah sat on a stone bench under a eucalyptus tree in the east barbican. In one hand he held the book, in the other, a writing slate, which he glanced at nervously from time to time. A sparrow chirped cheerfully in the branches overhead.

"Read the next line," Sir Faithful instructed.

Josiah looked up from the slate with a mournful expression on his handsome features. "Isn't it time for my instruction in swordsmanship?" he pleaded.

The old steward laughed and scratched at his long beard. "Not for another hour yet," he replied. "You are doing quite well in your use of the sword, Prince Josiah. It is your reading that is wanting."

"But it is so hard," the boy protested. "I struggle to remember the sounds of the letters, and I read so slowly!"

"Aye, but that will improve with time," Sir Faithful said patiently. "And your learning to read is so very important!"

"Why, sire?"

"King Emmanuel gave you the book that you might know him," the old man replied. "The book is your guide for life. It not only tells of your King; it can also guide your path. You must learn to read, and read well, if you would be a faithful servant of your King."

Josiah sighed. "Forgive me for complaining, sire. It's just that we've been at this all morning, and my mind is weary."

The white-haired old man stood to his feet. "Let's take a brief recess from your lessons, then. Perhaps a walk would clear the cobwebs from your head."

As Josiah placed his slate on the bench and stood to his feet, the old man suddenly wheeled and drew a sword on him. Josiah's own sword slashed through the air, meeting steel with steel to repel the blow. "Well done, my prince," Sir Faithful said, beaming with approval. "You have learned well." He lowered his blade.

"And you have taught well, sire," the boy responded. He laughed suddenly. "You know, Sir Faithful, when you first started teaching me the use of the sword, I thought that you were too old to fight well, or to teach me anything. But I still have much to learn before I could hope to wield a sword against you."

The old man smiled as he sheathed his sword. "No one is ever too old to serve King Emmanuel. Some of His oldest warriors are among the best." He looked Josiah over. "You have gained weight in the few weeks that you have been here. You have filled out nicely!"

"I weigh more than seven stone now," Josiah said proudly. "I weighed only five-and-a-half when I first came to the Castle of Faith." He laughed. "No one can be undernourished for long if he eats regularly at the King's table!"

It had been just five short weeks since Josiah had been set

free from Argamor's Dungeon of Condemnation and become a prince. During his brief stay at the Castle of Faith, daily exercises in horsemanship, sword handling, and reading and writing had taught him much, and he was well on his way to becoming a valiant warrior for the King. Through it all, young Josiah's love for King Emmanuel had deepened and grown.

Castle life was far better than anything that he could have imagined. The Ecclesia, or residents of the Castle of Faith, were all in various stages of growth and development, but they all had one thing in common—a deep, abiding love for their matchless King. Josiah spent time talking with every person in the castle—from Lord Watchful who protected the castle to the lowest scullion in the kitchen—and he soon knew them all by name. He basked in the love of King Emmanuel and his people, and the wounds of the past healed quickly.

The young prince paused. "Sire, there is something that I must do before another day passes."

Sir Faithful studied his face. "And what is that, Josiah?"

"In my limited reading of the book I have learned that when King Emmanuel was here, he allowed another to dip him beneath the waters of a river. I have also noted that in the second section of the book his followers did the same. Should I not also do that, since I am following him?"

The old steward smiled. "His Majesty's words have spoken to your heart, my prince. Your King would be honored if you would follow him in this way. This ordinance is called 'immersion.' Do you understand its significance?"

Josiah frowned. "I'm not sure, sire. Explain it to me."

"Immersion in water is an act of obedience to your King, for his book commands it for his followers," Sir Faithful explained. "The act itself is symbolic of Emmanuel's death for you."

"How, sire?"

"When a follower of Emmanuel is placed beneath the water, it symbolizes the King's death and burial. When the follower is raised from the water, that symbolizes His Majesty's victory over death when he came to life again. In the same way, the follower dies to the old life and rises to live a new one."

Josiah nodded. "I think I understand. May I do it now, in the Sea of Conviction, before another day passes?"

The old man smiled. "There is no better time, my prince."

A short while later, as the young prince and the castle steward emerged from the waters of the Sea of Conviction, they looked up to see many of the residents of the Castle of Faith watching from the shore. "My heart is full, Sir Faithful," Josiah said joyously, "for I have obeyed my King. And now I am ready to serve His Majesty."

Sir Faithful strolled across the barbican and climbed the steps leading to the sentry walk. Josiah walked beside him. "Where did the book come from?" Josiah asked. "How did we get it?"

"King Emmanuel commissioned more than three dozen men to write it. The writing took place in a number of regions, and took a millennium and a half to complete."

"So ordinary men wrote it, sire?"

"Aye, lad, but each and every word was carefully supervised, and the writing came out flawlessly. The book is completely accurate and without error. The first division of the book tells the history of Terrestria before the coming of King Emmanuel, and the second division gives the history after he came." He looked at Josiah. "Study the book, my prince. Your King will speak to you through the pages of the book, and he will reveal his plans and desires for you. It is only through the book that you will learn to serve His Majesty faithfully."

"King Emmanuel will speak to me through the book?" the young prince asked, with a look of awe on his eager face.

The steward nodded. "It is through the book that His Majesty has chosen to reveal his will for you. As you read the book and learn to obey it, King Emmanuel will guide you and direct you. Then your life will be pleasing to him."

"I want that more than anything else!" Josiah exclaimed earnestly. He paused, and a wistful look crossed his face. "I just wish that there was some way that I could speak to the King."

Sir Faithful looked surprised. "There is a way, my prince. Did you not know?"

Josiah shook his head.

The old man held out his hand. "Give me your book." Josiah pulled the volume from within his doublet and handed it to his friend, who opened it to the last page. As Josiah watched, Sir Faithful lifted a small parchment from the book. Written across the top of the parchment in bold script were the letters "P-R-A-Y-E-R."

The young prince stared at it. "What is that?"

"As a child of the King," Sir Faithful replied, "you have the right to send a petition to His Majesty at any time. Let me show you how to do it."

"Sire, what is P-R-A-Y-E-R?" Josiah interrupted, pointing to the letters at the top of the parchment.

"Providential Resources Attending Your Every Request," the old man replied. "Any time you wish to send a message or request to your King, simply write it on this petition, and it will be delivered immediately to His Majesty at the Golden City."

Josiah was puzzled. "How?"

Sir Faithful smiled. "I'll show you. Is there a message that you would like to send to His Majesty right now?"

Josiah's face lit up with delight. "There certainly is!" He thought for a moment. "I'd like to thank him for setting me free from Argamor and from my chains, and I'd like to thank him for adopting me into his family."

The old man handed him the parchment and a quill pen. "Then why not send the message to him right now?"

The young prince took the parchment and began to write, laboriously spelling out the words of the following message:

> *"My King,*
>
> *Thank you for freing me from my chans and from the evel blaksmth. Thank you for leting me be a prins in yur famly. I will serv you forever.*
>
> > *Yur son, Josiah."*

He looked up at Sir Faithful. "There. I just hope that King Emmanuel can read my writing."

The old man smiled. "He will understand you perfectly. Send it to him."

"How do I do that, sire?"

"Roll the parchment up and then release it," Sir Faithful replied.

Josiah rolled the parchment tightly and then gave the steward a puzzled look. "What do I do now?"

"Just open your hand, my prince, and see what happens."

Josiah did, and to his astonishment, the tightly rolled parchment shot from his hand and disappeared over the castle wall faster than an arrow from a longbow. He stared after it. "What happened to it?"

"Your petition is now in the hands of His Majesty," Sir Faithful answered, his eyes twinkling with amusement at the look of astonishment on Josiah's face. "He has received it already."

The idea was almost more than the young prince could comprehend. "You mean that the parchment has already reached the Golden City?" he blurted, shaking his head as if he just could not believe it. "Sire, that's—that's incredible! How could it travel that fast?"

"Any petition you send to His Majesty will reach him in an instant," the old man replied softly, "and he receives and welcomes every one of them. Prince Josiah, any time that you have a need or a request, or simply want to communicate with your King, you may send a petition."

"But where will I get another parchment like that one?"

"Look in your book." The young prince did, and to his surprise, found a parchment identical to the one he had just sent. "You will never be without a petition," the old man explained, with eyes twinkling. "There is no limit to the number that you can send. In fact, your King delights in hearing from you in this way. I dare say that the petition you just sent brought a thrill of delight to His Majesty's heart."

"Then I should send petitions often," Josiah remarked. He closed the book and placed it within his doublet. "Suppose that I have a need, or suppose that I desire an answer to a question?" he asked. "Will His Majesty send a petition back to me?"

Sir Faithful laughed. "He will answer you, lad, but not in that way. Sometimes he will speak to you through your book. Sometimes he will send someone to help you or guide you."

"Can I ask him for anything?" Josiah asked eagerly. "Anything at all?"

"There are some things that you might ask for that would not be good for you, or do not fit into His Majesty's plan for you. In those instances, he will answer 'no'."

Josiah was thoughtful as he and Sir Faithful climbed the castle stairs. "This whole matter of sending petitions to His Majesty is simply amazing," he declared. "I'm going to send him another tonight and tell him that I love him." He turned and looked at the old steward. "Will that thrill King Emmanuel's heart?"

Sir Faithful nodded. "I'm sure that it will, my prince."

They had reached the battlements of the northeast tower just then, and Sir Faithful leaned out into the crenel, placed his elbows on the stone ledge, and rested his chin in his hands. From their elevated position in the tower he and Josiah could see a great distance across the moors and forests. The old steward stood quietly for several moments, gazing off into the distance.

"What are you looking for, sire?" Josiah inquired.

"I can see a score of furlongs from here. I was watching the roadway and hoping to see King Emmanuel returning."

Josiah gazed expectantly up the roadway. "Is he coming back today?" he asked anxiously.

"He might. I hope he does."

"But didn't he tell you when he will come?"

The old man shook his head. "He didn't tell anyone."

"What about Lord Watchful? Doesn't he know?"

"King Emmanuel didn't tell any of us exactly when he's coming. He just gave orders to occupy the castle until he comes, and to be ready at any moment."

Josiah felt a warm glow as he thought about the King's return. "Won't it be grand," he said aloud, "having King Emmanuel here in the castle with us?"

"Oh, he won't stay here," Sir Faithful told Josiah, turning to look at him. "He's just coming back to take us away."

"Take us away? Away to where?" Josiah couldn't imagine any place as grand as the Castle of Faith, and he was disappointed at the prospect of having to leave.

"To the Golden City of the Redeemed, of course. He's preparing places for us there right now, even as we speak. The City of the Redeemed is our eternal home."

"Sir Faithful?" Josiah was hesitant to ask the next question. "Do you think that the Golden City of the Redeemed will be as delightful as the Castle of Faith? Will we be as happy there?"

The old man smiled at the boy's earnestness. "When you have read the book, you will know the answer to that question."

"But sire, I need to know now."

"I won't make you wait, lad. But allow me to answer you in this way. Our King built Terrestria, beautiful as it is, in just six days. The Castle of Faith was built in three days and nights. King Emmanuel has been working on the City of the Redeemed for nearly two thousand years. Does that not tell you anything?"

The young prince thought it through. "Then the Golden City must be absolutely splendid!" he decided.

"Oh, it is, lad, it is. The street of the City is made of pure gold. The walls are of jasper, with foundations of gems. There are twelve gates, each made from a solid pearl. The river of life flows through the center of the City, and there will be no more death, pain, or sorrow of any kind. Best of all, we'll be with King Emmanuel forever! Now, does that sound as if the City of the Redeemed is as grand as the Castle of Faith?"

Josiah's eyes were wide. "Aye!" he exclaimed. "It sounds far grander!"

Sir Faithful laughed. "I didn't even tell you the half of it, Prince Josiah. The City of the Redeemed is far grander than either of us could ever imagine." He turned away from the battlements. "Come on; let's get back to the reading lesson, shall we?"

Josiah's heart was full as he followed the steward down the winding stairs in the tower. "I've decided that I like being a prince. It's far better than being a slave, any day! I'd much rather get to do what I want to do than to be ordered around all day. Aye, the life of a prince is the life for me."

Reaching the battlements on the east wall, they crossed the sentry walk, passed through a door, and descended three flights of stairs. "I feel rather sorry for those poor scullions in the kitchen," Josiah continued. "All day long, the cook orders them about as if they had no rights of their own. 'Do this! Don't do that! No, not that way, you drudge, do it this way!' I'd get mighty weary of that. Who wants to be a servant when he can be a prince?"

He was surprised when Sir Faithful walked right past the bench beneath the eucalyptus tree. "Sire, where are we going?"

The old man stopped at the well in the bailey. "Draw me a bucket of water, Your Highness," he said stiffly, handing the wooden bucket to Josiah. "Then wait for me here."

Puzzled by Sir Faithful's actions, Josiah took the bucket and stared at the old man's back as he disappeared through a doorway. Dropping the bucket into the well, Josiah turned the windlass and slowly lowered it down to the water. When the bucket filled he cranked the windlass and winched the bucket back up.

As he pulled the bucket over to the side of the well, Sir Faithful reappeared with a basin and a towel. "Fill the basin," he ordered. Josiah complied and then set the half-full bucket on the stone wall of the well.

The old man handed him the towel. "Wash my feet," he ordered.

Josiah stared at him. "What?"

"I have been walking in the moors outside the castle this morning, and my feet are dirty. Wash them for me."

Josiah laughed. "I am a prince, remember? I had a hard time

getting used to the idea at first, but now I rather like it. And princes don't go around washing other people's feet."

"Prince Josiah, are you better than your King?"

The question shocked the boy. "Of course not, Sir Faithful. Why do you ask that?" Josiah saw tears in the old man's eyes, and suddenly he knew that he had made a very tragic mistake, but he wasn't quite sure just what it was. He waited anxiously.

"When you first came to the Castle of Faith, Prince Josiah, you had the heart of a servant. Your heart was full of wonder at the grace of your King, and you saw yourself as being unworthy to be invited into his castle. Had I asked you to wash my feet that first day, would not you have done it gladly? But now, you see yourself as being too good, too important, to do the job of a servant. You have mocked the kitchen scullions because they are servants and have to take orders all day."

Josiah hung his head. "I didn't mean it that way, sire."

"King Emmanuel is the King of kings and Lord of lords, yet he has the heart of a servant. One night His Majesty took a basin of water and some towels and washed the feet of his followers to show them what servanthood really is. If King Emmanuel is not too great to be a servant, then surely servanthood is good enough for you and me."

Josiah studied the old man's face. "King Emmanuel actually did that? He actually washed their feet?"

"You can read about it in your book. The story is found in the second section."

He smiled sadly. "Oh, Josiah. You were not saved from the Dungeon of Condemnation to be important or to become great, my prince. You were saved to be a servant, though you are a prince. Your chief goal in life should be to glorify your King."

Josiah bowed his head. "Forgive me, Sir Faithful. I shall wash your feet now. I want to be a servant like King Emmanuel."

But the old man shook his head. "Not now, Prince Josiah. It wouldn't mean as much now."

Chapter Nine

Winter passed quickly, and warm weather came to the Land of Terrestria. The moors and the meadows were bursting with color and the trees of the forests came alive with new greenery. Songbirds heralded the coming of spring as butterflies danced in the warm sunshine.

Prince Josiah and Sir Faithful walked single file down the narrow path across the crest of the hill, dodging branches and forcing their way through dense undergrowth in places where the path all but disappeared. The indistinct trail crossed a small stream, and the man and the boy traversed it by jumping from one steppingstone to another. The trail wound its way up the side of a rocky hillside, becoming progressively steeper and more treacherous as they walked.

Josiah used his hands and feet to scramble up a steep embankment. A projecting spur of rock broke loose when he trusted his weight to it, and he tumbled a short distance to the bottom. "How much farther?" Josiah called, dusting himself off and retrieving his walking staff. He hurried to catch up to his friend.

"We've got a long day ahead of us yet," Sir Faithful replied.

He turned, and, realizing that Josiah had fallen behind, waited for him to catch up. "This is the Forest of Decision," he told the young prince, "and it's not a friendly place after dark."

Josiah leaned his staff against a tree and paused with his hands on his knees, trying to catch his breath. "I can't believe how quickly you can still move for—" He hesitated, searching for the right words.

"For an old man?" the steward finished with a laugh. "You may be young, lad, but you will have to keep putting one foot in front of the other to keep pace with me."

Josiah nodded. "I know, sire," he puffed. "I'm finding that out."

"Can you tell yet why we couldn't take the horses?"

"They'd never make it up this pathway," Josiah said, eyeing the hillside above him. "I'm really not sure that we can, either. It looks like it gets even steeper ahead."

"Our path will level out after a time," Sir Faithful assured him. "It's not all this rough."

"The forest certainly is dark and gloomy here," the boy observed. "The trees are so thick that the sunlight can barely get through."

"Be thankful that we have a sunny day. If it were overcast, we could hardly see the trail. Now if you have caught your breath, we should be off. We have at least twenty furlongs yet ahead of us."

"I'm ready." They climbed in silence. Just as Josiah had feared, the trail soon grew steeper.

The boy's Breastplate of Righteousness was coming loose and

striking against his ribs with every stride. He paused to tighten the straps. Sir Faithful, apparently unaware that he had stopped, kept right on hiking.

Josiah struggled to untie the knot that fastened the breastplate at the bottom. The knot was behind him, and he fumbled with it unsuccessfully for two or three minutes. Finally, he grasped the armor with both hands and twisted it sideways, moving the breastplate around so that it slid to one side, covering his left shoulder. *There. Now I can at least see the knot.*

Gripping the troublesome knot with his fingernails, he tried again. The knot was tight, but he worked at it relentlessly. He was unable to loosen the knot by pulling on it, so he grasped the straps on each side and attempted to push them into the knot and thus loosen it. Twisting back and forth repeatedly, he continued to push on the thongs. The knot loosened, and moments later, he had it free.

Twisting the breastplate back into place, he hastily retied the leather straps. There. That was better. He retrieved his walking staff and started forward. It was then that he realized that Sir Faithful was out of sight. The forest was dark and the undergrowth was dense, but as far as he could see, the hillside above him was deserted. "Sir Faithful!" he called, "wait for me!"

"For me!" the forest echoed, throwing his words back in his face to taunt him. "For me! For me!"

He tried again. "Sir Faithful! Please wait!"

"Wait! Wait! Wait!" the echo replied.

"Sir Faithful!" Josiah scrambled up the trail, forcing his way through the bushes and briars that reached for him as if determined to slow his progress. "Sir Faithful! Wait!" Lowering his head, he charged up the mountainside, running as hard as he could. He tripped over a root and fell, cutting his hand and scraping his knees. Afraid to stop, he leaped to his feet and fought his way forward.

Moments later he stopped and looked around in confusion. The trail was gone. The undergrowth was so thick he could hardly force his way through, and there was no evidence of a path. "Sir Faithful! Where are you?"

"Are you? Are you?" the forest mocked him.

Panic threatened to overtake him, but he fought it off. "The trail can't be far," he reasoned, talking out loud just to hear his own voice. "I'll just backtrack until I find it again, and then I'll be on my way. Sir Faithful can't be too far ahead."

Heading downhill again, he found the going much less strenuous. *I think the trail is this way,* he told himself when he came to an area where the undergrowth was thinner and the walking was easier. *It can't be far now.*

He paused to catch his breath and heard a strange clanking sound coming from across the hillside. The noise was as if someone had put a number of cooking pots into a large bag and was shaking them about. *How strange,* he thought, *but it has to be another human being.* He hurried toward the sound.

Moments later he came upon the source of the unusual noise. A tall, blond-haired man with long muttonchop whiskers was hiking merrily along. Battered pots and pans of every shape and size were tied to the pack on his back, clanging and banging with every step. But he was on the trail.

"Sire, can you help me?" Josiah called, stepping from the bushes onto the trail. "Is this the right path?"

The traveler stopped and stared at him in surprise. "That depends on where you are going," he replied, giving Josiah a strange look.

Josiah walked closer. He could now see that the man's face was wrinkled and lined, although he moved with the energy of a much younger man. "I am Prince Josiah from the Castle of Faith, and I have lost my way. Can you help?"

"I am Palaios, the tinker. I make, sell and mend pots and pans. Are you looking for a quality cooking vessel? Perhaps a skillet?"

"Paloss? Paliess?" Josiah echoed, trying to pronounce the man's name.

"Palaios," the tinker corrected him. "It's from the ancient language. But maybe it would be easier if you would just call me 'Pal'. I like that just as well."

"Pal," Josiah repeated. "Can you tell me if I am on the right path?"

"That depends on your destination," Pal replied. "Where are you going?"

"We're going to the Village of Indifference," Josiah said brightly. "But we're only going to visit. We don't plan to stay. Sir Faithful wants me to see how the villagers live, because he says it will teach me something."

"We?" Pal echoed, looking around in confusion. "I see only one of you. Are you not traveling alone?"

"There are two of us, but I got separated from my friend and I lost the trail. I figure if I can find the trail again, I will meet up again with Sir Faithful."

The tinker nodded. "That makes sense. Allow me to show you the way." Josiah and Palaios started walking along the trail as they talked, and within moments, they came to a fork in the path.

Josiah stopped. "Which way?"

Palaios immediately pointed a long, bony finger. "That way." He indicated the path to the left, which angled downward at a rather steep angle and then disappeared around a sharp bend. "I must leave you at this point, but have a pleasant journey."

"And you're sure that this is the right path?"

"Of course. Trust me. In fact, this is a shortcut that will get you there much sooner than you had expected." The tinker turned away to take the other path.

"Wait, lad!" a voice shouted. Josiah and Palaios both turned at the interruption. A dark-haired young man with a longbow in his hand and a quiver on his shoulder came dashing down the trail. He was clad from head to toe in green, and was obviously a hunter. "Is this man giving you advice or counsel?"

"I just asked him for directions," Josiah replied.

"Don't listen to a thing he says!" the newcomer shouted, waving his arms about as if to emphasize the urgency of his warning. "This man will lead you astray."

"Who are you?" Josiah asked, puzzled by the hunter's excitement.

"I am Neos," the man in green replied, "and I say again, don't listen to this man."

"The lad didn't ask for your help," Pal told him curtly. "Be on about your business."

"Where are you going?" Neos asked.

"I'm trying to find the Village of Indifference," the young prince declared, "but I've been separated from a very good friend of mine and I've lost my way."

"Wherefore would you want to go to the Village of Indifference?" Neos inquired. "There's not much for you there."

"In a way, I'm on an errand for the King," Josiah replied, beginning to wish that neither man had come along so that he could be on his way and catch up to Sir Faithful. "A friend of mine is taking me there to teach me something."

Neos nodded at the explanation. "Then take this path," he said, pointing to the trail that led uphill. "But beware when you arrive in the Village of Indifference, for the town is not a healthy place to visit."

"This is the way!" Pal shouted, pointing to the downhill path. He shot an angry look at Neos. "Be off with you, knave, and leave the directions to me."

"He's leading you astray," Neos warned, stepping closer to Josiah. "Take no heed to what he says. You want the path to the right."

"The path to the left!" Palaios shouted. "Now leave the lad alone!" He shook his fist in Neos' face. "Be gone with you."

"And I say to cease leading the lad astray." Neos replied. "I know these woods like the back of my own hand. The lad wants the path to the right."

"The left."

"The right."

"The left!"

"The right!"

At that point, Palaios took a flying leap and landed on Neos, knocking him to the ground. The two men tumbled over and over, fighting furiously. The tinker's pots and pans clattered and clanked as he fought, raising a horrible racket that echoed throughout the woods. Josiah stood breathlessly watching the spectacle before him.

Neos pulled free of the tinker's grip and struggled to his feet. But the tinker grabbed him by the ankles and pulled him down again. He began punching the younger man as hard as he could, again and again. Neos blocked his punches and began throwing some of his own. Fighting furiously, the two men rolled over against Josiah, who hastily scrambled out of their way.

The young hunter was clearly getting the worst of it, and Josiah felt sorry for him. "Come on, Neos," he called, "don't let him beat you! Thump him! Harder! Harder!" To his amazement, at that instant the tide turned and Neos began to prevail. Within moments, he had managed to flip Palaios over on his back. Sitting astride the older man, he grabbed the hood of his tunic and began to shake his opponent with all his might.

Josiah saw no reason for the ferocity of the hunter's actions, and he called, "Neos! You have him under your power! Why not let him be?"

Suddenly Palaios twisted over, grabbed Neos by the throat, and threw him bodily to one side. Springing to his feet, he leaped on the hunter and began to pummel him mercilessly. In a flash, the tall tinker had again seized the advantage.

The fight went back and forth time after time, with first one man and then the other getting the upper hand. Josiah called out encouragement to the hunter when he was getting the worst of it; and then rooted for the tinker when it looked as if he was getting a beating. Never did he notice that whichever combatant he sympathized with immediately began to dominate; never did it occur to the young prince that he actually had control of the outcome. The hunter and the tinker fought and fought, thrashing around through the undergrowth, hurling each other about, throwing and receiving punches repeatedly without growing weary.

Josiah was considering taking his walking staff and joining in the fray when a loud, ferocious roar stopped him in his tracks. He whirled about. Like an apparition from a nightmare, a huge black bear rose above the bushes! With an angry roar that shook the forest, the furious beast charged out of the brush, heading straight for him! Dropping his staff, Josiah turned and ran. His heart pounded with fright.

The path to the right was closest, and the terrified boy followed it without thinking, though it led uphill. He ran as hard as he could, leaping over fallen logs that lay across the path, scrambling over boulders, plunging through briars. He ran until he thought his lungs would burst. Finally, when he could run no further, he fell to the ground behind a log, waiting with pounding heart for the enraged bear to catch him.

He listened, but heard nothing. The forest was silent; the bear was gone. He lay still for several moments, catching his breath, and then stood slowly to his feet. He glanced around him. He was standing in a huge patch of thick ferns. Gigantic trees lay rotting upon the ground like fallen soldiers from some long forgotten battle. The forest was sparser here, allowing more sunlight to strike the earth, and the atmosphere was bright and cheery.

Josiah cupped his hands to his mouth to call Sir Faithful, and then thought about the bear. With a sigh, he dropped his hands. Better to be lost than to be eaten by a bear.

He surveyed his surroundings, suddenly realizing that he had no idea from which direction he had come. There was no path. He glanced at the sun to get his bearings and then remembered that he and Sir Faithful had not been able to see the sun in the darkness of the forest. Checking the position of the sun now would give him a sense of direction, but would not tell him in which direction to head.

The position of the sun did tell him one thing, however: he was almost out of time. Night was coming fast, and he was alone, lost on the side of the mountain with no way of finding his way home to the Castle of Faith. What was it that Sir Faithful had said less than an hour ago? "This is the Forest of Decision, and it's not a friendly place after dark."

Chapter Ten

Darkness descended over the Forest of Decision as quickly as if it had been poured from a flask. Prince Josiah sat on a huge log as he tried to figure out what to do. He was lost, with no idea in which direction the castle lay, or how to go about finding it. The situation was hopeless. He dared not try to find his way in the darkness.

He thought about Sir Faithful. "Where are you, sire?" he said aloud. "I need your help." His thoughts turned to the book. What was it that Sir Faithful had said? "When you need direction, turn to the book. It will guide you."

Josiah drew the book from inside his doublet and stared at it in the darkness. In the black of night, the book was just a shadowy form; it would be impossible to read its pages. Josiah made a slashing motion with the book, transforming it into a sword. "I don't need a sword," he said aloud, "I need a light." He held the sword against his side, changing it back into the book again, and then tucked it back inside his doublet.

The moon came out at that moment, brightening the mountainside somewhat with its silver beams. Josiah reached for the book again. He held the volume in the moonlight, but the light was still too dim to see it well. Disappointed, he opened the pages of the precious volume. In the pale illumination from the crescent moon, the pages were indistinct and difficult to see. With a sigh, he closed the book.

"What will I do now?" Josiah said aloud. "I can never find my way off this mountainside in the darkness." *A petition!* The idea struck him like a bolt from a crossbow. Now would be the time to send a petition to King Emmanuel. He opened the back cover of the book and pulled out the small parchment, then closed the book and replaced it within his doublet. Lacking a quill to write with, he used a stick to scratch a simple message: "King Emmanuel, I am lost. Josiah."

The young prince held his breath as he rolled the parchment tightly and then opened his hand. Like an arrow from a longbow, the petition shot from his hand with a streak of light and disappeared over the treetops. He let out his breath in a long sigh. "I have sent my petition," he said aloud, "but how will King Emmanuel answer?"

"Use the book," a quiet voice seemed to say, and Josiah looked around in surprise. But the night was dark, and he saw no one. The words had been spoken so softly that he really couldn't tell whether he had heard an audible voice, or whether he had simply heard the voice in the inner chambers of his mind.

"Who's there?" he whispered timidly, but there was no reply. Josiah waited in silence.

"Use the book," the same quiet voice repeated. Glancing nervously around, the young prince drew the book from within his doublet and opened it across his knees. He waited, looking fearfully about in the darkness, but there were no further instructions. The voice was silent.

Josiah glanced downward, and was astounded to see that the pages of the book were glowing with a soft white light. As he watched, the pages glowed brighter and brighter until they were blazing with a pure white light that was dazzling in its intensity. Josiah turned the book, and the glow from its pages illuminated the clearing around him.

His heart leaped. Here was the light he so desperately needed. "Thy Word is a lamp unto my feet, and a light unto my path," he quoted. Standing to his feet, he began walking slowly through the ferns.

The book glowed brighter and brighter until its pages were illuminating the path for several paces ahead of him. Josiah went forward confidently, encouraged by the light. He entered the denser part of the forest and began to wind his way through the trees. It was then that he made an amazing discovery. When he turned the book in one particular direction, the pages glowed with an intense, bright light. But when he turned the volume in another direction, the light diminished and glowed feebly. The book was actually showing him which way to go—it was guiding him.

He walked faster, following the light from the book, using it to discern which direction he should take. Soon he saw a bright yellow glow through the trees ahead and he hurried toward it. The book shined brighter and brighter, reassuring him that he was on the right path. Moments later, he came upon a blazing campfire at the edge of a lean-to shelter built of logs. The delicious aroma of roasting meat drew his attention to a makeshift spit suspended over the flames. Seated before the fire was a familiar figure.

Josiah hurried forward. "Sir Faithful!"

The steward looked up with a welcoming smile. "My prince! You have learned to use the book, I presume."

The young prince laughed in relief as he closed the pages of the glowing volume. "It was indeed a lamp unto my feet and a light unto my path. I would never have found my way without it." He placed the volume inside his doublet and sat down beside Sir Faithful.

"I must beg your pardon," the steward said quietly. "When I planned this trial for you, I did not foresee the bear."

Josiah laughed. "He scared me out of my wits, I must admit." He picked up a stick and poked it into the fire. "I met two men, and they got into a fierce fight. They were—"

"Aye," the old man interrupted him. "I know. Palaios and Neos."

Josiah stared at him. "You saw them?"

"I not only saw your encounter with them; I planned it."

"Planned it? How?"

"Why do you think that your breastplate came loose?" the old man asked with a mischievous twinkle in his clear blue eyes.

Realization dawned upon the boy. "You loosened it," he accused, "so that I would stop and fix it, and you could leave me."

"Only so that you would meet Palaios and Neos," Sir Faithful said gently. "I was close by the entire time so that you would come to no harm." He chuckled. "But I didn't plan on the bear. Palaios and Neos made so much noise that the sleeping bear couldn't take the racket any longer."

"Why did you want me to meet Palaios and Neos?"

"The tinker did not tell you his surname. His full name is Palaios Anthropos, which is an ancient name meaning 'old man'. Neos' full name is Neos Anthropos, and his name means 'new man'."

"So they are brothers?"

"Not at all," the steward replied, "though they share the same surname."

"So why did you want me to meet them?" Josiah asked again.

"When King Emmanuel saved you from the Dungeon of Condemnation, he gave you a new nature. This new nature desires to please and glorify your King. But you still have your old nature, which is selfish and rebels against serving King Emmanuel. Each and every day, you must decide to which of your natures you will yield."

Josiah thought it through. "What would have happened," he asked slowly, "if I had followed the path that Palaios had wanted me to follow?"

"I would have done everything in my power to keep you from following that path," Sir Faithful told him, "because it led to a precipice from which you would have fallen. Palaios Anthropos is a treacherous individual; you must never trust him."

"I hope I never see him again!"

The old steward smiled ruefully. "I'm afraid that you have not had your last encounter with Palaios. He will plague you until you reach the Golden City." He reached for the spit on which the meat was roasting. "Let's eat and then get some rest, shall we? Tomorrow we shall continue our journey to the Village of Indifference."

An hour after sunrise the next morning, Prince Josiah and Sir Faithful approached a small village at the foot of the mountain, situated on the banks of a slow moving river. To Josiah's surprise, the stone wall surrounding the town had not been completed, and was only waist high. Piles of stone lay here and there in the weeds, abandoned along with rusting stone mason's tools, as if the wall builders had simply lost interest. In places, the wall was crumbling and falling down, and in others, it was missing altogether.

Josiah stared at the decaying wall. "This wouldn't keep anyone out," he told Sir Faithful. "Why didn't they finish building it?"

The steward smiled sadly. "In the next few minutes you will see why the wall was never finished."

Together the man and the boy strolled through the town gate, stepping carefully over piles of rubble and rotting timbers. Scraggly chickens ran about in the road, clucking and squawking irritably as they darted around huge holes in the cobblestone pavement. Grunting pigs rooted through piles of rotting garbage and refuse that lay in the street. Josiah held his nose. "This place has a foul odor."

He studied the humble houses that lined the narrow street, appalled at the condition of the tiny dwellings. Walls were cracked and crumbling; chimneys were falling down; thatched roofs were caving in. Doors and shutters hung precariously from broken hinges, or were missing entirely. Refuse littered the yards. In the center of the street, an open sewer ditch swarmed with flies. The wind howled mournfully through the branches of trees, barren in spite of the arrival of spring. The atmosphere in the neglected village was that of decay and death.

Josiah turned to his companion in disgust. "What is our business here, Sir Faithful? Can't we leave this dreadful place?"

The steward shook his head. "There is a lesson to be learned here, my prince. We must stay until you have seen that for which we have come." He led the way down the loathsome street, stepping carefully to avoid the worst of the filth and clutter.

Josiah had been watching for the residents of the Village of Indifference, but up to this point had seen no one. The entire hamlet seemed to be deserted. They reached the wall on the opposite side of the village, and Josiah realized that they had passed through the unsavory little town without seeing a single soul. "Where are the villagers, Sir Faithful?" he asked. "We haven't seen anybody."

"They are here," the old man replied, striding determinedly down the lane, "though you have not noticed them." He pointed. "There is one yonder."

Looking in the direction that Sir Faithful indicated, Josiah saw a sleepy figure in the doorway of one of the hovels. He stared at the man in surprise; the morning was young, and yet the man was sleeping. Glancing about, he began to spot villagers sleeping under trees and shrubs, huddled under decaying farm wagons, and sprawled in doorways. He even saw a young man sprawled upon the thatched roof of his house, sound asleep. He glanced at Sir Faithful. "Is the entire town asleep?"

"Nay, my prince. There are others whom you shall meet shortly."

At that moment, Josiah heard a rumbling noise like thunder, and several large boulders tumbled into the street. Josiah looked up in alarm. The mountainside loomed over the village, terminating in a sheer slate cliff that towered a hundred feet above the wall. As Josiah watched, several more boulders broke free and crashed down into the street. A portion of the bank suddenly crumbled away and slid down toward the village in a confusion of boulders, dirt, and small bushes. The landslide stopped just short of the village wall.

"That whole mountainside looks as if it could come crashing down upon the village at any time!" Josiah cried in alarm. "Where are the people? We need to warn someone!"

"There's the reeve now," Sir Faithful said, pointing to a figure advancing toward them. "He's in charge of the village, and his name is Sir Neglect."

Josiah ran toward the man. As he got close, he saw that the reeve's clothing was tattered and dirty. He was unshaven and in desperate need of a bath. A foul stench surrounded him, overwhelming the young prince.

"Sir Neglect!" Josiah shouted, grasping the man's sleeve in his excitement. "The mountainside is crumbling! The whole thing could come crashing down upon your village at any moment. You must warn the inhabitants of the village!"

Sir Neglect looked at him with filmy, lifeless eyes. "Why are you so agitated, my young friend? Calm down and relax. It's a beautiful day for a sailing."

Josiah pointed at the treacherous cliff that threatened the existence of the village. "The rocks are falling, sire! I just saw a small landslide. Your village is in danger, sire, and someone must warn your people!"

The reeve glanced up at the cliff and then back at Josiah. He smiled nonchalantly. "Don't be troubled, lad. If the mountain should fall, some of us would undoubtedly survive." He ambled away.

"Wait, sire!" Josiah started after the man, determined to impress upon him the seriousness of the danger threatening the town, but Sir Faithful grasped his sleeve.

"Let him go, lad. He will not listen to you."

"But someone has to warn the villagers," Josiah protested. They're in extreme danger!"

The old steward sadly shook his head. "This is the Village of Indifference, my prince. The townspeople will not hear you, either." He nodded with his head toward the river. "Come along, now, there is more that you must see." He led Josiah to the brink of the clay bank overlooking the river.

Prince Josiah looked down to see a huge crowd of men, women, and children assembled on the bank below him. Dressed in dirty, tattered clothing like Sir Neglect, the peasants were clustered at the water's edge, eagerly watching the river and shouting and cheering excitedly. In the middle of the crowd, two women were slapping each other and screaming insults, while a small group around them was urging them to fight. Downstream a short distance, two men fought in the shallows, each trying to hold the other's head under water. No one paid them any attention. Josiah stepped to the very brink of the bank and peered down at the noisy throng. "What are they doing?"

"You are watching a sailing race," the old man answered soberly. "The villagers make tiny boats from the reeds that grow along the water's edge, and then they race them down the stream to see who has built the fastest boat."

Josiah stared at him in astonishment. "That's what this excitement is all about? The villagers get this excited over little reed boats?"

Sir Faithful nodded sadly.

"But this is child's play!" Josiah exclaimed. "What does it matter who has the fastest boat?"

"The villagers think that it is important. Some of them spend all day, every day, building and racing the little reed boats."

Josiah shook his head. "This is the most foolish thing I've ever seen. These people should be building their town wall, and repairing their houses, and—and doing something about the mountain that is slowly falling on their village. They're in danger! Their children are in danger! But they're busy building foolish little boats."

"You are learning the lesson for which we came," Sir Faithful said softly.

"I can warn these people that the mountain is falling upon their village," the young prince said suddenly. He cupped his hands to his mouth. "People of the Village of Indifference! Hear me! The mountain is coming apart, and is falling upon your village! Your children are in danger! Leave the village and take your children to a place of safety!"

To Josiah's dismay, not a single soul looked up or acknowledged his warning. "They didn't even hear me." He cupped his hands to his mouth again.

Sir Faithful put a hand on his arm. "Save your breath," he advised. "They didn't want to hear you."

"Who are these people?" Josiah questioned. "Where did they

come from? And how have they gotten into this sorry state of affairs?"

"Believe it or not, these people are subjects of King Emmanuel. If you were to ask any one of them, he or she would claim loyalty to His Majesty. In fact, every person here used to dwell in the Village of Dedication."

Josiah looked at him in astonishment. "The village by the Castle of Faith?"

Sir Faithful nodded. "Some of them used to dwell in the castle itself."

"What happened to them? If they used to live in the Village of Dedication and they served King Emmanuel, why would they want to leave there and come to this dreadful place?"

The old man sighed. "Perhaps they grew weary in their service to their King. Perhaps they simply forgot what King Emmanuel had done for them and somehow lost the wonder of their deliverance. I don't know how it happened, but it did. One by one, these people chose to leave the blessings of the Village of Dedication and come to this place of apathy and indifference. They now lead empty, useless lives, and, as you can see for yourself, they are not happy."

Josiah shook his head as he watched the villagers leap about in their childish fervor over the little reed boats, fighting and squabbling with each other. "Why would anyone want to come to the Village of Indifference? It's such a dreadful place."

"I don't suppose that anyone ever *plans* to come here, but, as you can see, it has happened to many. It could happen to anyone. Anyone at all."

"Oh, it would never happen to me," Josiah assured him. "I

love King Emmanuel, and I love living in the Castle of Faith, and I love serving our King. I would never come here to the Village of Indifference. When we leave here, I never want to come here again. Nay, this would never happen to me. Not in a thousand years!"

"Don't say that, my prince," Sir Faithful pleaded. "This could happen to anyone. You should not say, 'This will never happen to me'. Rather, you should say, 'With the help of King Emmanuel I will stay faithful and never come to the Village of Indifference again.'"

Josiah watched the villagers as they raced about on the riverbank below, totally absorbed in their empty, frivolous boat races, oblivious to the danger that threatened their families. Two of the villagers engaged in a heated argument over the outcome of a race, and the rest of the townspeople began to take sides. "How sad," the young prince whispered. "How empty."

Sir Faithful took him by the arm. "You have seen that for which we have come," he said softly. "Let's head back to the Castle of Faith."

Chapter Eleven

Prince Josiah sat astride a powerful white horse in the shadows of the castle gatehouse. The handsome steed pulled at the bit and stomped the ground, eager to start moving. Josiah held him back.

"You have a flask of water and provisions for your trip," Sir Faithful told him, "so there is no need to stop to eat or drink. When you reach the Castle of Unity, the steward will see that you are properly cared for tonight, and will give you provisions for your return journey tomorrow." He handed Josiah a small parchment. "This is your map; it will guide you to the castle."

The young prince nodded. "I will be careful to follow it."

The old man then handed him a larger parchment, stamped with the seal of King Emmanuel. "This is a message of instruction and encouragement for the residents of the Castle of Unity. It must reach the castle by nightfall." He glanced at the sun. "If you will ride without delay, you will easily reach the castle before sundown."

Josiah took the parchment and tucked it carefully inside his doublet. "I shall not fail you."

"This mission is not for me, my prince; it is for King Emmanuel himself."

"I shall not fail my King, sire."

Sir Faithful gripped his arm. "Prince Josiah, I remind you—you must reach the Castle of Unity before nightfall! It is imperative that the parchment be delivered before the sun goes down. Remember, the King's business requires haste."

Josiah nodded and gripped the reins. "I shall not fail my King, sire. The parchment shall be delivered to the Castle of Unity ere the sun goes down in the west." He shook the reins, and the horse leaped forward. The clatter of hooves on the drawbridge echoed across the morning air.

Josiah watched the townspeople as he rode through the Village of Dedication. Men, women, and children scurried about, busy in the service of their King. The looks of contentment on their faces told him that their lives were fulfilled and satisfying. The young prince couldn't help but contrast them with the empty, frivolous lives of the inhabitants of the Village of Indifference. "Help me, my King," he whispered, "to never lose the wonder of what you have done for me, or to become like the people in the Village of Indifference."

The young prince rode steadily for several hours, glancing from time to time at Sir Faithful's map to be certain that he was following the right road. The sun was bright and his heart was light. He sang songs of praise as he rode, delighted to be on an errand for his King. When the sun was high overhead, he paused beside a quiet stream to rest his horse and eat the provisions from his saddlebag.

The clatter of hooves arrested his attention and he looked

up from his meal to see a mounted knight approaching. The man was arrayed in dark armor. Josiah stood to his feet anxiously with his hand upon the book, ready to draw the sword if necessary.

The knight reined to a stop less than five paces from where Josiah stood. He drew a short sword. Josiah responded by drawing his own sword, and the glittering blade caught the bright sun.

The stranger flipped back the visor of his helmet, and Josiah saw dark eyes that glittered with amusement. "I come in peace, my lord," the knight said, lowering his sword. "My name is Relevance." He looked with amusement at the huge weapon in Josiah's hand. "You have quite a sword there, my lord. It appears to be quite cumbersome and heavy."

"It was provided by my King," Josiah replied, slashing the air to show his ability with the weapon. "It suits me fine."

"Would not you care to have one that is less cumbersome and heavy?" the knight pressed. "I have one that is lightweight, yet sharp and effective in battle." He extended his sword to Josiah. "Here. Try it for yourself."

Josiah stepped close to the horse and took the sword from the knight. The weapon was nearly a foot shorter than his. It was lighter, and the jeweled handle felt good in his hand. He swung the sword a few times to get the feel of it.

"Pleasant, is it not?" the dark knight said. "It is so much easier to handle than the long blade that you are carrying. This lighter sword will not weary you in battle like yours would."

Josiah looked longingly at the smaller sword. The jeweled handle and shiny blade glittered and sparkled enchantingly in the bright sun, drawing the young prince mysteriously to it. He found himself wanting the beautiful jeweled weapon. "How could I get a sword like this?"

The knight hesitated. "This sword is valuable to me, my lord, but I suppose that you might talk me into trading for your sword." He stopped and held up one hand as if he had changed his mind. "Nay, nay, I beg pardon; I must change my mind. I cannot part with this sword."

Josiah held his own sword up to the knight. "I am willing, if you will trade."

The dark knight paused and seemed to be thinking it through. Josiah waited anxiously. "Aye, my lord," Relevance said finally. "This fine sword is yours; I will make the trade." He handed the short sword to the boy and took the much longer one.

Josiah swung the new sword, enjoying the feel of the jeweled handle. "I thank you, sire."

The knight lifted one hand to his visor. "My pleasure, my lord." Turning his horse, he rode away, taking Josiah's sword with him.

The young prince held the new sword against his side, but it did not change into a book like his other one did. Unsure what to do with it, he tucked it under the cantle of his saddle, wondering if he had made a good trade after all. He walked back to the stream and finished his meal.

Less than an hour after making the stop for his noonday meal, Josiah found himself riding along a narrow roadway bordered on both sides by forests of tall oaks, poplars and willows. In a small clearing just about a furlong ahead, he could see a humble farmhouse surrounded by a split rail fence.

"Greetings, my lord."

Josiah reined to a stop and looked around, trying to discover the owner of the voice. A peasant dressed in a dirty, threadbare jerkin stepped from the woods and hurried to the roadway. His eyes were wide as he gazed in wonder at the magnificent horse and Josiah's fine clothing. "Begging your pardon, my lord, but I could use your help for a moment or two. Would you spare the time?"

"What do you need?" Josiah asked pleasantly, trying not to show impatience at the delay. "I am on business for the King."

"My name is Distraction, and I need your help," the man told him. "One of my chickens has escaped, and I can use your help in catching it."

"The King's business requires haste," Josiah replied, quoting Sir Faithful, "and I must be on my way. Perhaps another can help you with your chicken."

"This will just take a moment of your time, my lord," Distraction replied with a beseeching look on his thin face. "Please help."

The young prince hesitated. Indeed he was on business for Emmanuel, and yet, somehow, he found it difficult to resist the pitiful farmer's pleas. "Just for a moment, then," he agreed, climbing down from the saddle and throwing the reins over a nearby bush. "Where is this chicken?"

"She went into the woods about here, my lord," the farmer told him, leading the way into the forest. "I've been chasing her all morning, but perhaps the two of us can corner her quite quickly."

Josiah and Distraction pushed their way through the dense weeds and undergrowth as they searched for the errant chicken. The woods were dark and gloomy, and Josiah peered anxiously about. "What color was the chicken, sire?"

"She was white, my lord. She should be quite easy to spot."

The young prince and the farmer searched unsuccessfully for nearly half an hour. The missing hen was nowhere to be found. Josiah suddenly remembered that he was on the King's errand. "I must leave you, Distraction," he told the farmer. "I am on business for His Majesty, and I must hasten on."

"My lord, don't leave me," the farmer begged. "I pray you, stay just a moment longer. This chicken is precious to me, my lord, and we must find her."

Josiah could not resist the pleading look in the man's eyes, and he reluctantly agreed to stay. "All right," he promised, "but just another minute or two. I really must be on my way."

They searched unsuccessfully for several more minutes. "I must leave—" Josiah began, but the farmer cut him off.

"There she is, yonder. We found her!" He rushed forward, and Josiah felt compelled to follow.

The chicken was hiding under a thicket and as the prince and the farmer approached, she exploded from her hiding place and half flew, half ran through the woods, squawking loudly. Josiah and Distraction gave chase. They ran as hard as they could, dashing around trees and crashing through thickets in pursuit of the elusive hen. Their feathered foe continued to evade them, darting forward like a bolt from a crossbow each time they had her within reach.

They chased the fugitive fowl for more than an hour, following her deeper and deeper into the forest. Finally, Josiah managed to corner the bird against an outcropping of rock. But as he reached for her, she fluttered up into the branches of a tree. "Can you climb for her, my lord?" the farmer begged. "At my age, I don't dare."

Josiah obligingly began to climb the tree. The chicken flapped her wings and scrambled higher. The boy soon found himself twenty feet above the ground. As he reached for the chicken, he glanced across the forest. His heart sank. The sun was dropping rapidly toward the hills to the west. There was less than an hour of daylight left.

The prince seized the hen by one wing. "Got you!" Pulling the reluctant fowl to him, he tucked her inside his doublet and climbed down quickly. "Here," he said, thrusting the runaway chicken into the farmer's hands. "I must get back to my horse and get on with His Majesty's business."

Josiah felt a pain in his heart as he hurriedly tried to retrace his steps through the forest. He watched the setting sun while he scrambled toward it, dodging trees and bushes as he ran. With a growing sense of dismay, he realized that the night would overtake him long before he reached his destination. *You should never have stopped to help Distraction,* he chided himself. *You will never make it to the Castle of Unity before the sun goes down! His Majesty's business should have come first. Sir Faithful told you that the parchment must reach the castle before nightfall. You have failed your King.*

Filled with remorse, Josiah ran faster. His heart was pounding and his lungs were burning by the time he reached the roadway. He burst from the woods and glanced at the sky. His heart sank. The sun was quickly sinking behind the trees on the other side of the road. Night was coming fast.

He ran to the bush where he had left his horse. To his alarm, his steed was gone. He looked up and down the roadway in desperation, but the horse was nowhere to be found. A flash of silver reflected the rays of the dying sun and he hurried over to it. The sword he had received from the unknown knight lay in the dust, and he stooped and picked it up.

"Forgive me, my King," he whispered contritely. "I have failed you, my Lord, and have not completed my mission for you." The pain in his heart was increasing. Filled with remorse, he set off down the road on foot.

Moments later the sound of pounding hooves caused him to turn around. His heart leaped with fear. Bearing down on him at full gallop were two knights in black chain mail!

Josiah leaped to the side of the road. Gripping his sword tightly, he stood ready to defend himself. One knight spurred his horse forward and raised his lance. Josiah raised the sword to repel the blow. The lance came flashing down, and Josiah met it with the blade. To his horror, the lance bent the blade of the sword as if it were a reed! Josiah stared in dismay at the ruined weapon. The lightweight sword was worthless!

He felt the cold edge of steel against his neck. "Don't move, knave!" a harsh voice commanded.

The knight with the lance dismounted, threw Josiah face down to the ground, and bound his hands behind him. His captors jerked him to his feet, and then raised the visors on their helmets. Josiah gasped in alarm. The two knights in black chain mail were none other than Evilheart and Lawofsin!

Evilheart laughed at the expression of disbelief that appeared on Josiah's face. "Glad to see us, my lord?" he taunted.

"Untie me!" Josiah demanded, when he had recovered from the shock of coming face to face with Argamor's henchmen. "You have no power over me. I am a prince, heir to King Emmanuel Himself."

Lawofsin laughed and bowed low. "Forgive us, Your Highness," he mocked. "We didn't realize that we were in the presence of royalty."

"Untie me!" Josiah demanded again. "I am no longer the slave of Argamor and he has no power over me. I now serve King Emmanuel and have been adopted into his Royal Family."

"Save your pleading for the ears of Lord Argamor," Evilheart growled. "It is at his orders that we have seized you."

"But Argamor has no power over me!" Josiah protested. "I no longer serve—"

"Silence!" Lawofsin roared. "Not another word from you!"

Evilheart lifted Josiah and threw him over the front of his saddle, then mounted quickly. The horse leaped forward into a gallop. With each stride the young prince was thrown about and bounced painfully up and down against the pommel of the saddle. *Where are they taking me?* he asked himself in terror. *How can they do this to me? Don't they see that I am a prince?*

An hour later, his belly was sore from the constant pounding when the horsemen finally reined up in front of a formidable gate. Josiah lifted his head, and despair swept over him. His captors had brought him back to the Dungeon of Condemnation!

Chapter Twelve

Prince Josiah's heart pounded with fear as he looked up at the entrance to the Dungeon of Condemnation. His mind immediately recalled the countless nights of torment in the darkness of that dreaded place, and he recoiled in horror. At that moment an overwhelming sense of hopelessness and despair overwhelmed him, crushing in its intensity, so complete and so dreadful that it seemed as if he could not breathe.

"Are you not glad to be back, Your Highness?" Lawofsin mocked him, pulling him from the saddle and standing him upon his feet. "Welcome home, knave."

The two men dragged him to the gate of the dungeon. Evilheart banged on the gate with the hilt of his sword, and a guard that Josiah had never seen before came and unlocked it. A feeling of desperation swept over Josiah as Evilheart and Lawofsin dragged him through the gate, down to the lower level through the iron gate, and into the inner ward. They took him to the dismal cell that he had occupied before and he noted that the damaged bar had been replaced. *This can't be happening!* Josiah's heart cried out. *I don't belong here! I've been set free!*

The men pounced on him and tore his breastplate away and

then removed his belt. Lawofsin grabbed his cloak and ripped it from him. Evilheart seized his doublet and ripped it to shreds, tearing it from his body. Josiah was in tears as they snatched the shoes from his feet and even pulled the King's ring from his finger. When they had finished, he was standing barefoot on the cold, damp floor, clad only in the robe that the King had given him.

Both guards were grinning broadly as they pushed him into the darkness of the cell and locked the door. "It's good to have you home again, Your Highness," Lawofsin sneered, and both men laughed mockingly.

An overwhelming sense of dread seized Josiah as the footsteps of the two guards echoed down the empty corridor. He gripped the iron bars of the cell. "Wait!" he screamed, "I don't belong here! There's been a mistake! I belong to King Emmanuel—he set me free!" In answer, laughter rang through the corridor, echoing and re-echoing to mock and torment him.

Josiah sank to his knees. It had all happened so quickly. One moment he was Prince Josiah, heir to King Emmanuel, enjoying the blessings of being a member of the Royal Family. In the next moment he was a prisoner, locked securely back in the Dungeon of Condemnation.

The parchment! My Assurance parchment will prove that I really am a prince, and that Argamor has no right to hold me here! But as he reached for the parchment, he knew already that the precious document was not there. Not only had he lost his sword and his ring, he had lost his parchment as well.

Moments later heavy footsteps sounded in the corridor as several men approached the entrance to the inner ward, and Josiah's heart filled with terror. Before the gate even opened he knew who was coming. He dropped his head in abject defeat.

"On your feet, wretched knave!" the hateful voice roared, and Josiah looked up to see the fearsome figure of Argamor at the bars.

"M-my lord!" The words were out even before Josiah was aware that he was saying them. He sprang to his feet, trembling in terror. Argamor glared at him with hatred blazing in his evil eyes.

"So, lad, you thought that you might escape, did you?" Argamor's cruel laugh rang throughout the dungeon. "You are mine, knave! Mine! You are mine forever, and now not even your King can set you free! You are mine forever!" He threw back his head and roared with heartless laughter.

"My lord," Josiah gasped, hesitantly approaching the bars. "My lord, there has been a mistake! I am now a prince! I belong to King Emmanuel, and you have no right to keep me here!" Even as he said the words, his heart filled with terror at the rage upon Argamor's face.

"You were a prince," Argamor roared, "but no longer! You have betrayed your King, and you are mine again! You have failed, lad!" His eyes glittered with a cruel hatred as a triumphant leer crossed his features. "You are mine forever!"

"But I had a parchment from the King," Josiah argued, surprised at his own boldness. "It decreed that I was adopted into King Emmanuel's Royal Family forever!"

"Where is this parchment?"

"I-I lost it, sire," the boy stammered. "But I-I had it once, and it was s-signed and sealed by the King Himself!"

"Is this your parchment?" Argamor roared, unrolling a document and holding it up to the bars.

Josiah could see just enough in the dim light to recognize the parchment. He sprang forward eagerly. "Aye! That is it!"

"Be it known to all men everywhere,'" Argamor read aloud, "'that from this day henceforth, Josiah Everyman, of the Village of Despair, has been adopted into the Royal Family of King Emmanuel and shall henceforth and until such time as this document is revoked, be known as Prince Josiah, heir with King Emmanuel.'"

"It says 'forever'," Josiah protested, "and it says 'eternal'. You did not read those parts!"

The huge man scanned the parchment. "It says no such thing, lad." He looked hard at Josiah. "Can you read?"

Josiah nodded. "Aye."

"Then, wretched one, see for yourself!" Argamor thrust the parchment at him.

Josiah took the precious document with a trembling hand and held it up to the dim light. To his great dismay, the wording on the document was exactly the way that Argamor had read it. "But sire, it said 'forever'," Josiah protested. "I know it did!" His eyes dropped to the bottom of the parchment, and his heart sank. King Emmanuel's signature was no longer there, and His royal seal was missing.

Argamor seized the parchment from Josiah's trembling fingers. "You are mine forever, knave," he gloated. "Welcome back to the Dungeon of Condemnation." He crumpled the parchment in his dirty fist and dropped it to the floor.

Josiah heard the metallic clank of a heavy chain, and remorse filled his heart as his former master entered the cell and fastened a sturdy shackle to his ankle. Forged to the shackle was a huge chain of iniquity, and at the other end, the heavy weight of guilt. Tears rolled silently down Josiah's cheeks and spattered on the cold stone floor.

"Welcome back, my prince!" Argamor sneered, locking the cell door. His laughter filled the corridor as he, Lawofsin, and Evilheart strode from the inner ward and headed for the upper level of the dungeon.

Chapter Thirteen

"Make haste, lad!" Argamor roared, looking up from the huge chain he was making on the anvil. Anger was written across his swarthy features. "You can work faster! Faster! Faster!" The muscular arm of the huge blacksmith brought the heavy hammer down in a mighty blow against the glowing iron link upon the anvil, and the sound rang across the darkness of the afternoon like a vesper bell. The man's lip curled in hatred as he watched the hapless slave boy. Reaching up with a dirty hand to scratch his thick, black beard, he snarled, "You shall work harder, knave, or you shall taste the lash again!"

"Aye, my lord," young Josiah replied wearily. "I shall work faster, my lord." Gasping for breath, he struggled to haul the cumbersome coalscuttle across the muddy workyard. A freezing rain slashed at his back and the biting north wind howled through his grimy robe, chilling his weary body. Reaching down with his free hand, Josiah grasped the heavy chain to relieve the weight of the iron shackle around his thin ankle. At the opposite end of the chain, a large iron ingot nearly half the boy's weight slid across the muddy ground.

The ache in Josiah's heart had increased until he could hardly bear it. "I failed my King," he wept quietly, struggling against the heaviness of the loaded coalscuttle and the weight of guilt. "I failed King Emmanuel. Oh, my Lord, forgive me!"

"Faster, knave, or you shall taste the lash!" Lawofsin loomed over him with his whip raised.

Josiah blinked back the tears and tried to summon the strength to move faster. He threw back his head to take a deep breath, noting that the branches of the trees overhead were still bare and lifeless. Spring had already come to the Castle of Faith and the Village of Dedication, but here in the Village of Despair, it was still winter. The freezing rain fell faster.

Struggling against the weight of the chain and the scuttle heaped with large chunks of coal, Josiah managed to reach the shelter of the shed. Dragging the weight of guilt across the stone floor, he approached the edge of the flaming forge and timidly moved within arm's reach of the burly blacksmith.

Setting the scuttle on the rock ledge at the edge of the forge, Josiah stepped up onto the ledge to empty his burden of coal into the glowing furnace. Smoke and heat from the forge billowed around him, burning his eyes and searing his lungs. The blistering heat from the open fire was agony. Josiah took a deep breath and struggled to empty the clumsy scuttle into the red-hot forge.

As he dragged the empty coalscuttle across the yard for yet another load, his thoughts returned to the happier days he had known at the Castle of Faith. "I was loved," he whispered to himself, and the tears of remorse started again. "I was free. I was a prince, a child of the King!" He choked back a sob. "But I failed my King, and I lost it all." He dropped to his knees in the filthy coal yard and began to load the scuttle.

Josiah's heart ached with guilt, loneliness and remorse as he worked through the long, exhausting day. *I failed my King,* he told himself again and again. The ache in his heart grew each time he thought about King Emmanuel, the Coach of Grace, and the Castle of Faith.

Finally, the long hours of cruelty were over and he was led to the Dungeon of Condemnation and locked into the darkness of his cell. "Pleasant dreams, Your Highness," the guard sneered. His heartless laughter rang throughout the dungeon as he walked away.

Josiah shivered as he once again pillowed his head in the lice-infested straw. It had been a fortnight now—two long, exhausting weeks of cruelty and abuse during the day, and loneliness and condemnation at night. He sighed. The worst punishment of all was the huge chain of iniquity and weight of guilt fastened to his ankle. Having once tasted freedom from the chain, he now found that he could hardly bear the shackles.

A faint sound in the corridor outside his cell caught his attention, and he quickly sat up. "Who's there?"

A shadowy figure stood outside the bars. "I can help you, lad," a gentle voice whispered.

New hope sprang into Josiah's heart. He leaped to his feet, grabbed the heavy chain, and pulled the weight of guilt noiselessly across the cold stone floor. His pulse quickened with anticipation as he approached the bars.

"Oh." His heart sank. The man in the corridor was Father Almsdeeds. Disappointment flooded over Josiah like a cascade of cold water dumped from a bucket.

"I am Father Almsdeeds, a man of the Church," the cleric

whispered gently. "I have the keys that will free you from this dreadful abode. Here—take them. This is the Key of Religion," he explained, passing a shiny golden key through the bars. "And this is the Key of Penance—"

"I know who you are," Josiah said coldly. "I tried your keys before. They didn't work! I was still a prisoner in the Dungeon of Condemnation!"

Father Almsdeeds seemed genuinely concerned by Josiah's statement. "But I don't understand," he said quietly, thoughtfully rubbing his chin. "These are the very keys I always use! I've given these same keys to many other folk as well!"

"But has anyone ever been able to use them to escape the Dungeon of Condemnation?" Josiah demanded bluntly.

Father Almsdeeds was perplexed. "I really don't know," he answered slowly.

"And why are *you* here, sire, if your keys can set a man free?"

"Of a truth, I really don't know," the cleric said again.

"Sire, I don't want your keys," Josiah told him. "They are quite useless, though they are beautiful and gave me false hope for a time." As Father Almsdeeds moved meekly down the corridor, Josiah was surprised to see that the cleric had a heavy chain fastened to his ankle. With a heavy sigh, the defeated youth sank to his knees in the pile of filthy straw.

A petition! What if I could somehow send a petition to King Emmanuel? If His Majesty knew that I was once again locked in the Dungeon of Condemnation, would he not make a way to set me free? Josiah's shoulders sagged as a tormenting thought came back to haunt him. *But I have failed my King. I am no longer a prince. Argamor has recaptured me, and I am bound to serve him again.*

He sighed. *And since I am no longer a child of the King, I have no right to send His Majesty a petition.*

Josiah's heart was heavy as he looked around the cold, dark confines of his lonely cell. "Perhaps it doesn't really matter anyway," he whispered aloud, bitterly, "for I no longer have my book, and therefore I have no parchment with which to send a petition."

His eyes fell upon the crumpled parchment that Argamor had hurled to the floor a fortnight before. His heart leaped. Perhaps... The lonely youth crawled across the cold stones and picked up the document with trembling fingers. Smoothing it out, he tore a long strip from one edge. He felt around in the darkness until he located a small, sharp stone. Smoothing the strip of parchment across his thigh, he used the stone to scratch a desperate message:

> *"King Emmanuel,*
>
> *I have failed you, and I am sorry. Please forgive me.*
> *I would do anything to become your son again.*
>
> *Prince Josiah."*

He pondered the words he had written, and then, with a heavy sigh, used the stone to scratch out the word "Prince". Rolling the despairing message into a tight roll, he shook his head. His eyes filled with tears. "It's no use," he whispered, though his heart ached within him. "King Emmanuel will not receive a petition from me, for I have failed him and am no longer a part of the Royal Family." Hot, bitter tears flowed freely down his cheeks as he opened his hand and allowed the scrap of parchment to fall to the floor.

To Josiah's astonishment, the petition shot from his fingers, and, in a thin streak of silver light, vanished from the cell! It seemed that it had passed right through the wall of the dungeon. His heart pounded fiercely as he stared at the cold, gray stones of the wall. Was it possible? Had King Emmanuel received his petition?

He waited breathlessly, his pulse quickening with anticipation, hope, and at the same time, fear. A rat emerged from a hole in the wall and scampered across the cell, disappearing under the edge of the door. Josiah scarcely noticed. *Will King Emmanuel receive my desperate petition? Will he free me from this miserable dungeon?*

But nothing happened. At last, Josiah sank to the straw and slowly closed his eyes, disheartened and bitter. There had been no reply from King Emmanuel.

Three nights later, after a particularly hard day at the cruel hands of Argamor, Josiah lay shivering in the darkness of his cell. He tried to go to sleep, but his thoughts once again kept returning to his golden days of freedom at the Castle of Faith. What happiness he had known! What joy, what peace he had experienced, knowing that he was a child of the King and that his iniquity and guilt were gone!

He sighed, remembering the joyous feasts he had enjoyed at the King's table in the great hall. The warmth of the fire on the hearth, the aroma of fresh-baked bread, the laughter of happy children, the love and fellowship of the other residents of the castle—the meals in the great hall had been divine. But all that was gone now and he hurt inside to even think of such things.

Oh, that I could attend just one more King's Supper, he thought wistfully. *What joy, what delight I experienced each time we gathered for that special time.* The King's Supper, a simple meal of unleavened bread and juice from the fruit of the vine, was a sacred event when the castle residents gathered to commemorate King Emmanuel's death for them. The juice, symbolic of the King's blood, and the bread, symbolic of his body, reminded them of the tremendous sacrifice their sovereign had made when he purchased their freedom.

"One of the things I miss the most," he said aloud, trying to quell the dreadful loneliness in his soul, "is the music. What lovely music we enjoyed during the feasts in the great hall!" In his imagination, he could almost hear the minstrel's golden voice as he softly strummed his lute and sang melodies of praise to King Emmanuel.

The words of one of the minstrel's songs went through his mind, and he tried to sing them.

"I sing the greatness of my King, my Lord Emmanuel
His power is great and far exceeds
What mortal tongue or pen can tell.
My heart is full; I sing for him,
And trust that I may serve him well."

As Josiah came to the last line in the verse, the song died in his throat and he fell silent. What was there to sing about in the Dungeon of Condemnation? He had *not* served his King well. He had failed miserably, had failed his gracious King, and the blissful days among King Emmanuel's loyal followers were gone forever. The pain in his heart intensified until he thought he could bear it no longer.

"Prince Josiah!" The whisper in the corridor was soft and gentle, but it came without warning and it startled him.

He sat up. The dim glow from the torch in the corridor silhouetted the figure of a man against the bars of his cell. "Are you Prince Josiah?"

"I am a prince no longer," Josiah answered coldly.

"But are you the prince?" The whispered voice was eager, insistent.

"I am Josiah, though I am no prince."

"His Majesty be praised! I have found you!" the mysterious visitor whispered. "I have searched high and low for you. Prince Josiah, I have been sent to get you out. I can help you."

"I want no help," Josiah replied. After the letdown he had experienced following the initial visit from Father Almsdeeds, he was not going to risk getting his hopes up again.

"Prince Josiah, I have come to help you," the visitor insisted.

"Go away!"

"Prince Josiah—"

"Leave me alone," Josiah retorted bitterly. "I am not a prince, and I do not desire your help. Now, leave me alone."

"But you do not belong here," the visitor insisted. "Prince Josiah—"

"Do not call me that!" Josiah exploded. "I tell you, I am not a prince! Princes do not slave all day carrying coal for the blacksmith's forge, and they don't spend their nights languishing in dungeons. I tell you, I am *not* a prince."

"Oh, but you *are* still a prince."

"I failed my King," Josiah replied bitterly. "I was distracted from the King's business and I failed in my mission. I lost a valuable horse. I lost my sword. I failed to deliver a vital message to the Castle of Unity, and I allowed myself to be captured by Argamor's cohorts, Evilheart and Lawofsin. I have failed, and I am no longer a prince."

"Failure doesn't end any relationship with King Emmanuel," the stranger said softly. "He adopted you into the Royal Family forever."

"That's what I thought," Josiah shot back. "But look." Stooping, he picked up the crumpled parchment from the floor where Argamor had tossed it earlier. Smoothing the document out, he thrust it toward the mysterious figure. "Read it for yourself, sire. It doesn't say 'forever'. I tell you, I am no longer a prince."

The man glanced at the parchment. "Where did you get this?"

"It was given to me by King Emmanuel," Josiah said slowly, "on the very day that He set me free. Somehow I lost it, and Argamor brought it here again."

"This is not the parchment that was given you by King Emmanuel."

Josiah looked at the man in surprise. "How do you know, sire?"

"His Majesty's signature and seal are not here," the man replied, pointing to the bottom of the document. "This document did not come from King Emmanuel."

"Then where *did* it come from?" Josiah challenged. "And how did Argamor get it?"

"Argamor is a liar and a deceiver. This is simply a clever

forgery. He copied the Parchment of Assurance that King Emmanuel gave you, but he left out certain parts to lead you astray. He wants to keep you as his slave, but he has no hold on you. Prince Josiah, I am come to show you the way out of the Dungeon of Condemnation."

Josiah's heart leaped at the words, but then doubt crept back in. "Who are you, sire?" he asked suspiciously. "Are you a friend of Father Almsdeeds?"

"My name is Sir Reconciliation," the visitor replied softly. "I was not sent by Father Almsdeeds; I was sent by King Emmanuel in answer to your petition."

Josiah wept softly.

He looked up in surprise as Sir Reconciliation appeared at his side. The visitor had entered Josiah's cell without even opening the door. "Prince Josiah, you do not belong in the Dungeon of Condemnation," the man said quietly. "I have come to help you return to the Castle of Faith."

"How do I know that this is true?" Josiah asked, weeping. "Sire, I have failed my King."

Sir Reconciliation put a gentle hand on his shoulder. He pulled a copy of the book from his bosom and opened it. The pages began to glow with a heavenly light that illuminated the cell. "There is therefore now no condemnation to them who belong to King Emmanuel..." he read quietly.

Josiah's head shot up. "No condemnation? Does it really say that?"

"Right here in His Majesty's own words," the gentle visitor responded. "You have the King's promise on it, Prince Josiah. There is no condemnation for you; therefore, you do not belong in the Dungeon of Condemnation."

Josiah wept with joy at the words. "But sire, how do I get out?" he asked. "The bars and doors are strong and I have no key."

"The Key of Faith is always found in the book," Sir Reconciliation replied. "These bars and doors have no power over you, my prince. Simply walk out and leave the Dungeon of Condemnation behind you forever!"

"If only it were that easy," Josiah replied, still weeping. "If only it were that easy."

"But it is, my prince," Sir Reconciliation told him. "The Dungeon of Condemnation cannot hold you. As a child of the King, there is no condemnation for you. Simply walk out of this dungeon by faith!"

"And what about the chain of iniquity, and the weight of guilt?"

"King Emmanuel set you free forever, Prince Josiah. The book says so." Sir Reconciliation turned the pages of the book. "Here it is. Listen to this." He read a passage promising eternal freedom from the chain of iniquity and the weight of guilt.

Josiah was amazed. "So I am free, sire? I can just walk out?"

Sir Reconciliation nodded. "It's that simple, Josiah. Argamor cannot hold you in this dungeon of his, because you have been set free forever by King Emmanuel."

Josiah shook his head. "I'd like to believe that, sire, but there's a heavy chain upon my leg. I can feel the weight of it. And there are bars—I can see them." He sighed. "How I wish that what you are saying were really true."

Sir Reconciliation leaned forward. "It is true, Prince Josiah," he said earnestly. "It's in the book, written by King Emmanuel, and His Majesty would never lie. He cannot lie. What I'm tell-ing you is the truth. If you will only believe it, you can be free! If you know the truth, the truth shall make you free.'"

"I wish I could know that. Sir Reconciliation, I have failed my King! And I'm afraid that means that I have lost my salvation, that I am no longer a prince."

"What is that upon your head?"

Josiah reached up. "Why, it is my helmet of salvation!"

"Exactly," Sir Reconciliation said, with a note of triumph in his voice. "Argamor and his henchmen took your parchment of assurance, and your shoes of service, and your ring symbolizing your relationship to the King. But they could not take your helmet of salvation, nor your robe of righteousness. They could take your assurance, and they did, but they could not take your salvation."

"But they took my ring," Josiah argued, "and my relationship to King Emmanuel."

"They took your ring, 'tis true, but not your relationship. The ring was merely the symbol of your relationship."

Josiah sat quietly thinking it through. "Then I—" he hesitated, afraid to voice the question he was longing to ask— "then I am still a prince?"

"Aye, Prince Josiah, every bit as much a prince as the day that King Emmanuel adopted you into the Royal Family."

Josiah hesitated. "I'm afraid to try," he said finally. "If it's not true, my heart shall not be able to bear the disappointment."

"Believe your King's word, Prince Josiah," Sir Reconciliation pleaded. "By faith, believe your King. Argamor has no power to keep you here. You are a prince forever, and the Dungeon of

Condemnation has no power over you."

He thrust the book into Josiah's hands. "Here. This is now your sword. Use it. Trust your King's promises and walk free this very night."

The young prince was trembling as he stood to his feet. "I will believe my King," he said softly, "because he would never lie to me. I will be free again!"

"Use the Key of Faith," Sir Reconciliation urged. "It is found within the pages of your sword."

Josiah reverently opened the book. To his astonishment, a golden key lay within, glowing with a warm, golden light. His fingers trembled as he picked it up.

Holding the book in one hand, he reached down with the key. The instant the key touched the shackle attached to his ankle, the chain and shackle fell to the stone floor with a crash that reverberated throughout the ward. The thrill of freedom swept through his soul. Striding confidently forward, Prince Josiah grasped the locked door of the prison cell. He inserted the Key of Faith into the lock, turned it, and easily pulled the door open. "I thank you, my King," he whispered, rushing to the locked iron gate and unlocking it.

Sir Reconciliation was at his side as he took the stairs two at a time and reached the upper level in triumph. His heart pounded with rapturous joy. Confident in the promises of his King, he hurried to the main gate.

The dungeon guard met him with a drawn sword. "Hold it right there, Your Highness," he sneered. "You are not going anywhere!"

Chapter Fourteen

The burly prison guard advanced toward Prince Josiah with a snarl of rage contorting his features. The blade of his sword reflected the feeble light from his torch. "Get back to your cell," he snarled, "before I run you through!"

Josiah hesitated, and his faith wavered.

"Use your sword, my prince!" Sir Reconciliation called. "He cannot stand before you if you use your sword."

With trembling hand, Josiah clutched the book and swung it in a wide arc. In an instant, a blade of polished steel cut through the air. "There is therefore now no condemnation," Josiah quoted, "to them who belong to King Emmanuel."

At these words, the menacing guard threw down his sword and bolted away through the darkness of the corridor. Sir Reconciliation turned to Josiah with a smile. "Open the gate, my prince, and walk out. You are a free man!"

As Josiah approached the main gate, the huge iron barrier opened of its own accord and swung to one side with the squeal of protesting hinges. With a shout of joy, Prince Josiah stepped outside. Sir Reconciliation was at his side.

"The victory is yours, my prince," Sir Reconciliation told him. "Go in faith, trusting in your King. And now, I must leave you. Make your way back to the Castle of Faith. A warm welcome awaits you there, I assure you."

"Sire, how will I find my way back?"

"Your book will guide you, Prince Josiah. Simply walk in its light."

Josiah seized his benefactor and hugged him. Tears of joy flowed down his cheeks. "I thank you, Sir Reconciliation. I am forever indebted to you for what you have done for me tonight."

"Thank your King," Sir Reconciliation answered. "He is the one who has provided the Key of Faith to set you free. Farewell, my prince."

Prince Josiah's heart was singing as he set off through the darkness. He walked quickly, determined to put as much distance as possible by daybreak between himself and the Dungeon of Condemnation. He clutched the book to his side. "I'm free!" he whispered gratefully. "Forever free!"

The roadway grew darker, so Josiah opened the book and allowed the light from its pages to guide him. Just as he had expected, the pages glowed with an intense white light that dimmed each time he turned to one side or the other. As long as the light glowed at full intensity, he knew that he was on the right path to the Castle of Faith.

He came to a fork in the road. Uncertain as to which direction to go, he held the book high and turned to the left. The book's pages began to dim; the light grew so feeble that he could scarcely see the roadway. He turned to the right.

The pages began to glow brightly again; the intense white light clearly illuminated the roadway to the right. Without hesitation, Josiah took the road to the right.

After traveling for several hours, the young prince crawled into a haystack at the edge of a humble farm. Clutching the precious book to his bosom, he curled up in the hay and closed his eyes. "I'm free," he whispered softly. "There is therefore now no condemnation to them who belong to King Emmanuel." Within moments, he was fast asleep.

The sun was just beginning to peek over the eastern horizon when Josiah crawled stiffly from the haystack, brushing bits of straw from his robe. He turned to find a peasant farmer watching him suspiciously. "What are you doing, lad?" the farmer asked.

"I am making my way to the Castle of Faith, sire," Josiah answered. "I stopped for a rest in your haystack."

A look of concern swept across the man's features. "The Castle of Faith is many furlongs from here," he said. "You have a long journey ahead of you. Here." He thrust a loaf of bread and a large wedge of cheese into Josiah's hands. "Sustenance for your journey."

After thanking the generous farmer, Prince Josiah continued his journey, munching contentedly on the bread and cheese as he walked. The sun was bright, and the day was warm. "I sing the greatness of my King, my Lord Emmanuel," Josiah sang. His heart overflowed with joy. As he sang the last line, "And trust that I may serve him well," he was overcome with emotion, and his voice broke.

The journey was long. By early afternoon, Josiah was weary and his feet ached from the many furlongs on the dusty road. He had finished the last of the bread and cheese, and he began to grow hungry again. Soon he found himself passing through a small village. He sniffed the air, enjoying the aroma of the rich foods that the merchants along the street displayed so attractively, and he found himself wishing that he could stop and purchase some. But he had no money and he walked resolutely on, sustained by the anticipation of his welcome at the Castle of Faith.

As he left the little town behind, a discouraging thought began to nag at his mind. What if he was no longer welcome at the Castle of Faith? True, he was free of the weight of guilt and the Dungeon of Condemnation, but one fact remained—he had failed King Emmanuel. What if Lord Watchful, aware of his failure, refused him entrance to the castle? What would Sir Faithful say?

His steps faltered as he thought about it, and he found himself walking more slowly. Sir Reconciliation had assured him that all would be well, but what if he were wrong? Josiah sighed. He would not know for sure until he actually reached the castle.

"Wait for me, my lord!" a pleasant voice called, and Josiah turned to see a cheerful little man in a golden tunic and green leggings. He was carrying a lyre under his arm. As Josiah waited in the roadway, the little man hurried to catch up with him. "If it pleases you, my lord, may I share the journey with you?"

Josiah's thoughts were still focused on the possibility of being rejected at the castle and he was in a melancholy mood. He really didn't care for company at the moment, but he answered stiffly, "It makes no difference to me, sire."

"I thank you, my lord," the little man said, beaming as if he had received a warm welcome. He took a deep breath as he fell into step beside Josiah. "My, what a wonderful afternoon! His Majesty's blessings are manifold, are they not?"

Josiah shrugged. "Aye, I suppose."

"My name is Encouragement," Josiah's new companion said. "I see from your countenance that you are downcast and worried. Might I play a melody for you on my lyre? It might lift your spirits."

Josiah shrugged again. "As you wish."

Encouragement began to strum the strings of his lyre and a peaceful melody flowed from the instrument, soothing and gentle as it floated across the countryside. To Josiah's astonishment, the little man began to sing a familiar song of praise. "I sing the greatness of my King, my Lord Emmanuel..."

Josiah's eyes filled with tears as he listened to the beautiful melody. Encouragement sang the entire song as they walked along. When he had finished, he paused in the roadway and looked directly into Josiah's eyes. "Young friend, why not tell me what is troubling you so? Perhaps my King can use me to be an encouragement to you."

"I am Josiah, and I have been told that I am a prince, although I do not look or feel like one." Without hesitation, Josiah told Encouragement the entire story of his adoption by King Emmanuel, his days of service at the Castle of Faith, and his failure on the King's errand. "I was on an important mission for the King," he said sadly, "but I stopped to help a peasant farmer catch a chicken, and look what happened. We caught the chicken, but I failed King Emmanuel. I was trying to do good but I failed in the most important business of all, and I disappointed my King!"

Encouragement nodded soberly, but his eyes were filled with compassion and understanding. "As servants to King Emmanuel, that is something we have to constantly guard against. Sometimes our adversary does not tempt us with evil; sometimes he allures us with something good to draw us away from that which is best, service to our King. We get so busy doing good things that we simply have no time for that which is best."

Josiah sighed. "Aye, that is what happened to me."

"Perhaps Argamor planned it that way."

The young prince looked at his companion in surprise. "Do you think that Argamor sent that farmer to distract me and draw me away from my mission for King Emmanuel?"

Encouragement smiled. "His name was Distraction, was it not? Without a doubt, he was sent by Argamor."

Josiah shook his head sadly. "I didn't know. I was just trying to do something good for someone else."

"That is a worthy motive, my young friend, indeed it is. But we must always guard against distraction from His Majesty's business. As I said, at times when Argamor cannot tempt us with evil, he will often tempt us with that which is good, in order that he might distract us from our service to Emmanuel."

Josiah then told of his capture by Argamor's men, of the grim days of servitude to the cruel blacksmith and the long nights in the Dungeon of Condemnation. He finished his tale with the account of his deliverance with the help of Sir Reconciliation.

"So, my young friend, why are you so downcast?"
Encouragement asked. "You are free. Argamor has no more
claim to you. Rejoice in the goodness of your King!" He began
again to strum softly on the lyre.

"But what if the things that Sir Reconciliation told me are
not true?" Josiah worried aloud. "What if I reach the Castle of
Faith and Lord Watchful won't let me in? What will I do then?"
He seized a fold of his own robe and held it up. "Look at me,
Encouragement. Do I look like a prince to you? I certainly do
not feel like one."

The little man paused in his strumming and looked Josiah
over from head to toe. "To be quite honest, my friend, you do
not look at all like a prince. Your robe is dirty and torn; your
feet are quite bare; and your face needs washing."

Josiah grimaced. "So you see what I mean."

"But you are still a prince, Prince Josiah," Encouragement
declared. "When King Emmanuel adopts one into the Royal
Family the relationship is eternal. The book promises that your
King will never forsake one of his own, never cast out one who
comes to him."

"But what about my Robe of Righteousness?" Josiah argued,
walking faster. "Look at it. It was given to me by King
Emmanuel, but now it's dirty and torn, and I've ruined it forever."

The roadway crossed a little wood and stone bridge spanning
a small stream, and Josiah and Encouragement walked across it.
Their footsteps echoed hollowly on the planks. The little man
paused in the middle of the bridge, took Josiah by the elbow,
and led him to the railing. "Lean over and look," he urged.
"What do you see?"

Josiah leaned over. "There's a little stream beneath the bridge," he replied.

"By what name is this stream called?"

"I do not know, sire."

"This is the Stream of Forgiveness," the little man told him. "It flows from the hill where King Emmanuel died for you. Walk into the water and see what happens."

Josiah left the bridge and walked down beneath it to the edge of the water. Placing his book carefully on the bank of the little stream, he stepped into the water, finding it quite cool and refreshing.

"Wade out a little deeper," Encouragement encouraged him. "Go in until the water flows about your shoulders." Josiah did. "Now come back out," Encouragement directed, so Josiah did.

"Look at your robe now," Encouragement instructed.

Prince Josiah glanced down at the Robe of Righteousness and gasped in astonishment. The garment was dazzling white, shimmering with iridescent blue highlights, spotless and clean and new. "It's clean!" the young prince exulted.

"So are you," Encouragement told him with a smile. "Prince Josiah, hear me. Your heart is full of love for your King, but I must warn you—you will fail Him again in the future. When it happens, you do not need a new robe; your robe simply needs cleansing."

Josiah examined the fabric of the robe, finding it new and unmarred in any way. "This is amazing!"

"Your King set you free forever, Prince Josiah. Go in faith to the Castle of Faith, and you shall find a joyous welcome awaiting you." Encouragement gripped Josiah's hand. "I must leave you now, my prince. I trust that I have been an encouragement to you. Farewell."

"I thank you, Encouragement. You have helped me greatly."

"A word of warning, Prince Josiah. Beware the Giant of Fear who lives in the Castle of Unbelief. He will do everything in his power to keep you from reaching the Castle of Faith. But remember, faith can overcome fear every time."

Josiah watched as the little man walked merrily up a winding path, strumming his lyre and singing a cheerful song of praise. When Encouragement had disappeared from sight over the crest of the hill, the grateful young prince turned and resumed his journey toward the Castle of Faith.

The afternoon shadows were growing long as Josiah trudged wearily up a steep slope. He had not seen a farm or dwelling of any kind for more than two hours, and he was beginning to wonder where he would spend the night. He came to a peaceful meadow shaded with tall oaks. Songbirds filled the air with their cheery melodies. Squirrels darted in quick circles among the trees, while others scampered about in the branches, jumping from limb to limb in one death-defying leap after another. Josiah laughed as he paused to watch their antics and rest his weary feet.

"Dreadfully sunny day, isn't it?" a thin, whiny voice declared. "Sunshine's so bright it nearly blinds the eyes."

"I rather like it, myself," Josiah replied, looking about in an attempt to find out to whom he was talking. "Sunshine warms the heart and lifts the spirits."

"Wretched birds, always singing and chirping," the same voice complained with a note of disgust. "If they carried the burdens men carried, they'd have nothing to sing about, I warrant."

Josiah looked about, still trying to locate the person with such a dismal outlook on life.

"Pesky squirrels! Always chattering and running about as if they owned the place. What a nuisance." Just then, Josiah spotted movement under a clump of gooseberry bushes, and a heavyset man dressed entirely in dark blue rose stiffly to his feet.

"Who are you?" he snapped, glaring at Josiah.

"I am Josiah, sire. Prince Josiah."

"Another prince!" the man in blue whined. "Too many princes in this wretched kingdom, I warrant." He glared again at Josiah. "What is your business here?"

"I-I'm just passing through," Josiah replied, a bit intimidated by the man's ill-tempered manners. "I'm on my way to the Castle of Faith."

"Why would you want to go there?" the man whined.

"Who are you?" Josiah challenged, beginning to get a bit irritated by the man. "And what is your business, sire?"

"My name is Doubting," the surly man replied, answering Josiah's first question and ignoring the second. "And as I was saying, you do not want to go to the Castle of Faith. Too much singing and laughter there, I warrant."

"But I *do* want to go there," Josiah protested. "The Castle of Faith is my home." Doubting was watching him with a suspicious eye, so Josiah felt compelled to explain himself. He told his story from beginning to end, exactly as he had told it to Encouragement.

When the tale was finished, Doubting began to laugh. "Take my word for it, lad, you do not want to go to the Castle of Faith. They will never receive you after what you have done."

"But Encouragement said that they would. I am still a prince, heir to King Emmanuel."

Doubting snorted. "Encouragement? Bah! What does he know? Just a foolish minstrel, he is. Take my word for it, lad, they will never receive you in the Castle of Faith."

"Why not, sire?" Josiah demanded hotly.

"You are a traitor to King Emmanuel," the stocky man said smoothly. "Would you consider it wise to allow a traitor to abide in the castle? Of course not! Lord Watchful will never open the gate to the likes of you."

"Well, I'm going anyway, in spite of what you say," Josiah declared. "Good day, sire." He turned on his heel.

"Lad, wait!"

Josiah turned to face him.

"I'm sorry if I have offended you," Doubting said in a quiet voice. "It was not my intention to discourage you, or cause you grief. I simply wanted you to know the truth." He stepped toward Josiah. "Allow me to help you."

Josiah was suspicious. "In what way?"

"Seeing you are so determined to go to the Castle of Faith, I might as well save your weary feet a few steps. There is a shortcut."

"Don't listen to him," a quiet voice warned.

Josiah looked around in bewilderment. "Who said that?" Seeing nobody, and hearing no answer, he turned back to the dour-faced man. "Where is this shortcut of which you speak?"

"Continue on your way until the road reaches the bottom of the hill," Doubting instructed. His voice had lost its whiny edge and now was smooth and reassuring. "You will see a valley on your left. Pass through the valley instead of following the road-way, and you shall save yourself thirty furlongs of walking."

"I thank you for your help," Josiah replied.

"The night is fast approaching, and it would not be safe for you to pass the night in the open. There are wild beasts that roam about at night. But there is a castle in the Valley of Dis— in the valley, and there you shall pass the night in safety."

"How shall I find this castle?" Josiah asked. "Are you sure it is safe?"

"Far safer than spending the night in the fields," Doubting assured him. "And the castle is easy to find—simply walk through the valley and you cannot pass by without seeing it."

Josiah hurried down the road, anxiously watching the sky. The sun was dropping fast, and night would soon be upon him. He was relieved when he came to the valley that Doubting had described, and without a second thought he hurried into it, following a narrow footpath that was almost overgrown with weeds and brush. The valley was dark and shadowy, the atmosphere forbidding. The air was foul and smelled of decay. Josiah glanced around anxiously. *What a dismal place,* he thought. Just ahead he saw the castle, nearly hidden in the purple shadows of night. He hurried toward it.

Moments later he found himself standing before a massive wooden gate with iron hinges. Tipping back his head, he stared in wonder at the entrance to the castle. The gate was nearly sixty feet tall.

"Why would anyone build a gate this big?" he wondered aloud. "It's as tall as a tree."

Just then the colossal gate swung open, and Josiah stared in astonishment at a huge pair of legs as big as tree trunks. He looked upwards, and his mouth fell open. Standing before him was a giant as tall as an oak tree!

Chapter Fifteen

Prince Josiah stared, hardly able to believe what he was seeing. The owner of the castle was more than thirty-five feet tall! The giant coughed, and the sound rumbled across the valley like peals of thunder, echoing and re-echoing until Josiah covered his ears to shut out the fearsome noise. The giant took two steps forward, and the ground shook beneath his massive feet. The young prince trembled, flattening himself against the edge of the walk in hopes that he would not be seen.

"Who dares to trespass on my land?" the giant rumbled, in a voice that boomed like a clap of thunder. He turned, and a boot nearly six feet tall brushed past Josiah, almost crushing the terrified boy. Josiah held his breath, afraid to move or breathe.

"Who's there, I say?" the giant rumbled again. Josiah thought his heart would stop.

The giant peered about eagerly, scanning the grounds outside his castle. The huge boot scraped the walk as the enormous man turned away from Josiah. The frightened boy crept noiselessly toward a boulder in the path, the only hiding place he could find.

A hand nearly four feet long seized him and in one quick swoop hoisted him more than thirty feet into the air! Josiah's stomach seemed to leap into his throat. He found himself face to face with a fearsome sight. Red hair framed a head that was almost as tall as he was. A curly red beard encircled a cavernous mouth. The nose was as big as a boulder. Below the nose was a thick moustache as wide as Josiah's outstretched arms. The eyes were terrifying—huge, glaring, and filled with resentment.

Clutching Josiah in one massive hand, the giant moved Josiah to within a few feet of his face. "One of the little people!" he boomed. "Insect, what are you doing here?"

"I came here by mistake—" Josiah began.

"Louder!" roared the giant.

"I CAME HERE BY MISTAKE," Josiah shouted. "NOW IF YOU WILL LET ME GO, I'LL BE ON MY WAY."

"Let you go?" the giant echoed. He began to laugh, shaking Josiah about without realizing it. "Insect, I want to have some merriment with you first!"

Josiah still clutched his book, but the giant's massive thumb pinned his arm against his side, preventing him from swinging it as a sword. The giant was squeezing him so hard that he could scarcely breathe. The young prince flexed his arms, pushing against the enormous fingers and trying to obtain a little breathing room.

"Why did you come here?" the giant asked, holding the struggling boy even closer. The giant's breath smelled of garlic and Josiah coughed and choked, struggling to breathe. "Why are you disturbing my solitude?"

"I was told that this was a shortcut—" Josiah began.

"Louder!" roared the giant.

"I WAS TOLD THAT THIS WAS A SHORTCUT!" Josiah shouted. "I WAS ON MY WAY TO—"

"I can't hear you," the huge man boomed, lowering his captive a few feet. "I'll take you inside, where I can hear you better." Stepping back through the gate, he closed it behind him and crossed the castle courtyard in huge, twenty-foot strides. He swung his arms as he walked, swinging the boy in his fist back and forth in long, dizzying arcs that made Josiah feel nauseous. After several moments, the terrifying ride came to an end as the giant entered the castle.

The giant opened his fist, allowing Josiah to tumble from his fingers to land on a hard wooden surface. Josiah scrambled to his feet, grabbing the book and tucking it under his arm in hopes that the giant hadn't seen it.

He stared at his surroundings in awe. He was in a huge room, a vast chamber even bigger than the great hall in the Castle of Faith. An enormous fireplace filled one wall. He looked up. Massive beams supported a ceiling sixty feet above his head. Realizing that he was standing on some sort of huge platform suspended above the castle floor, he crept to the edge and looked down. The floor was twenty feet below him. Suddenly he realized that he was standing on a table as big as a house!

Shaking with fear, Josiah backed away from the table's edge. His heels caught on a ledge and he fell backwards. As he rolled over and leaped to his feet, he found himself standing in the middle of an earthenware dinner plate six feet across. Feeling as small as a mouse, he crept to the edge of the plate and then saw the cause of his fall. He had stumbled over a five-foot knife.

"Here," the giant boomed, picking Josiah up and placing him inside an iron kettle that would have been large enough to bathe a team of horses, "now I will be able to hear you." He leaned down and peered over the edge of the kettle. "Who are you, and why are you disturbing my solitude?"

"I don't know what your solitude is, sire, and I didn't mean to disturb it," Josiah replied. His words echoed inside the iron vessel, amplifying the sound until it was so loud that it hurt his ears. But the look on the giant's huge face told him that his huge captor could now hear him.

"Why did you come here?" the giant asked again.

"I am Prince Josiah, and I am traveling to the Castle of Faith. I was told that this valley was a shortcut."

"Who told you?"

"A mean-tempered man I met this afternoon," Josiah replied. "His name was Doubting."

"You have met my brother?"

"Your brother, sire?" Josiah stared up in astonishment at the enormous face. "But you are six times as tall as he is!"

The giant shrugged. "So I got more than my share of the food when we were young. Indeed, Doubting is my little brother." He leaned closer and glared at Josiah. "Wherefore are you here on my property?"

"I was on my way to the Castle of Faith," Josiah began again.

"The Castle of Faith!" The giant roared with laughter, and the sound reverberated inside the iron kettle until Josiah worried that his eardrums would burst. "Insect, do you know where you are now? You are in the Castle of Unbelief!"

"The Castle of Unbelief? Are you the Giant of Fear?"

"I am indeed." A huge hand slapped the side of the kettle, knocking Josiah off balance and sending him crashing to the iron bottom of the vessel. "You shall never reach the Castle of Faith."

Josiah scrambled to his feet and turned to face the giant. "But I will, sire!" he retorted defiantly. "You shall never stop me!"

"Insect, do you think that your faith shall overcome my unbelief?" The laughter rumbled again.

"My faith is in King Emmanuel, and you shall never keep me from returning to the Castle of Faith!"

The Giant of Fear smiled smugly, and Josiah saw a neat row of three-inch teeth beneath the huge moustache. "I'm keeping you from it right now, Insect."

"But I'm not planning to stay long," Josiah retorted.

The giant suddenly reached into the kettle, plucking the book from Josiah's grasp with the tips of his colossal thumb and forefinger. "What's this?" Holding the book close to his face, he fumbled to open it. As he succeeded in opening the cover, the Key of Faith fell from the pages and landed on the table with a faint plink. The giant leaned down to look for it.

Josiah leaped upward and caught the rim of the kettle with both hands. Pulling himself up, he looked over the edge. He watched as the Giant of Fear managed to pick up the Key of Faith with his fingernails. "What is this?"

"It's my Key of Faith, sire."

"Your Key of Faith? It's so tiny." The giant laughed. "My fear is much bigger than your faith, Insect." He held the golden key aloft and examined it closely. "This little thing is hardly as big as..." He paused, trying to think of a suitable comparison. "It's hardly as big as a mustard seed."

"It's big enough," Josiah replied calmly. "It got me out of the Dungeon of Condemnation, and it will get me out of here!"

"Oh, I would doubt that," the Giant of Fear replied with a chuckle. He placed the key back inside the pages of the book, and then turned and tossed the book on the mantle above the fireplace.

Josiah's heart sank. The mantle was forty feet above the floor. He would never be able to get the book back. Overcome with disappointment, he released his hold on the rim of the kettle and allowed himself to drop back down inside.

"Supper is nearly ready," the Giant of Fear said, reaching into the kettle and plucking Josiah out. He placed Josiah on the table and then strode to the enormous fireplace to stir the contents of a huge pot. As he lifted the lid, a delicious aroma filled the room.

The Giant of Fear carried the steaming pot to the table and poured a vast quantity of the contents onto the six-foot dinner plate. A cloud of steam engulfed Josiah. As the giant returned the cooking pot to the fireplace, Josiah crept forward and stared into the plate. A thick, rich stew simmered in the plate, so hot that it was still bubbling and steaming. Josiah counted twenty-two whole chickens and thirteen whole geese floating in the broth.

A nine-foot loaf of bread slammed down beside the plate of stew, and Josiah leaped backwards in alarm as the huge knife slashed downward and sliced off a chunk. The giant dropped the knife to the table with a thunderous clatter. He pulled off a crumb of bread the size of Josiah's head and flicked it toward the boy with one finger. Reaching into the steaming plate of stew, he plucked out a chicken and sent it spinning in Josiah's direction.

Josiah stuck out one foot and kept the chicken from skidding past him off the edge of the table. Reaching down with both hands, he grabbed the fowl and discovered that it was too hot to pick up. He retrieved the chunk of bread, sat on the edge of a three-foot long candlestick holder, and waited for the chicken to cool.

The Giant of Fear picked up his huge plate, tipped it slightly, and then used his knife to rake vast quantities of the steaming stew into his cavernous mouth. Josiah saw him swallow two chickens at one gulp. In no time at all the plate was empty. The giant returned to the fireplace, retrieved the cooking pot, and poured another fifty or sixty gallons of stew into his plate.

When the simple meal was finished, the giant pushed his plate to one side. "And now for some music," he boomed. He stepped to the fireplace, retrieved a golden harp from the mantel, and returned to the table. Placing the harp close to the candlestick upon which Josiah sat, he asked, "Insect, do you play?"

The look on the giant's face told Josiah that he would not be pleased with a negative response, so the boy shrugged and replied, "I'll try, sire." Pulling the golden instrument closer, Josiah sat on the edge of the candlestick and placed his fingers upon the strings. Running one hand experimentally across the strings, he was relieved when the sound that resulted was fairly pleasant. Encouraged, he reached for the strings with both hands.

After several minutes of plucking and strumming and experimenting with the harp, Josiah sat back and lowered his hands. The last notes died away. "You play very well," the Giant of Fear rumbled, and Josiah looked at him in surprise. "Continue."

Josiah raised his hands to the harp, and, to his amazement, a familiar melody poured forth from the golden strings. Continuing to run his fingers lightly across the strings, Josiah listened intently, trying to recognize the tune that his fingers played so readily. He finally realized that he was playing the song of praise that he had heard the minstrel play in the great hall of the Castle of Faith.

As the beautiful song came to a conclusion, the amazed boy lowered his hands and glanced at his colossal captor. The Giant of Fear was sound asleep!

Josiah stood to his feet, and one huge eye cracked open. "Play it again, Insect," the giant mumbled. "Aye, it's beautiful." Once again, as Josiah played, the giant drifted off to sleep.

Josiah finished the song and sat quietly watching the giant. The huge chest rose and fell with a regular rhythm, and the rumbling snores told the boy that the colossal owner of the Castle of Unbelief was sound asleep. He rose quietly to his feet and crept to the edge of the table. Now was the best time to escape!

Josiah peered anxiously over the edge at the floor some twenty feet below. How would he get down without breaking a leg? Perhaps he could drop to the seat of one of the chairs and then slide down one of the legs. But that would make a terrible racket, and the sleeping giant would surely hear. There had to be another way.

"Going somewhere, Insect?" The booming voice scared Josiah nearly out of his wits, but he recovered in time to keep from falling off the edge of the table. The huge hand snatched him up. "I must find somewhere to keep you for the night."

The Giant of Fear walked to the cupboard with Josiah in his fist, selected a five-foot teakettle, and carried it back to the table. Twisting the lid from the teakettle, he plopped the boy inside it and then replaced the lid firmly. "Pleasant dreams, Insect," he said with a booming chuckle. Moments later Josiah heard him lock the castle door.

The inside of the teakettle was smooth as glass, and Josiah had a hard time standing. Bracing his feet against one wall, he pushed against the top with all his might, but the lid was unyielding. Finally, Josiah sank in frustrated exhaustion to a sitting position on the bottom of the teakettle.

Fear began to settle over Josiah like a cold, wet mist. *What if I never make it back to the Castle of Faith?* he worried. *What if the Giant of Fear decides to keep me here forever? I'll never see Sir Faithful again. I won't be at the castle when King Emmanuel returns. What if I never see my King again?*

Forgetting the promises he had read in the book, Josiah allowed fear and unbelief to take hold of his heart, troubling him deeply. He worried and fretted about his captivity, and wondered about the reception he would receive if he did make it back to the Castle of Faith. He finally fell asleep, curled up in the bottom of the teapot, despairing of ever escaping from the Castle of Unbelief and the Giant of Fear.

Late one afternoon, Josiah felt his teapot prison shake as the

Giant of Fear returned to the castle. He had been a captive of the giant for more than a week now. The giant had not been cruel to him, but he had kept him cooped up in the teapot every night and every time he left the castle during the day. Josiah also knew that the giant kept the castle door securely locked.

Josiah sighed as he heard the castle door swing open. "I'll never get out of here," he whispered in despair. "I'm locked in a teapot, with no way of escaping. The table is twenty feet high and I can't get down safely. Even if I could, the giant keeps the castle door locked, and I have no way of opening it." He fell silent as the lid of the teapot popped open and he found himself looking up into the colossal face of his captor.

"I ripped my sleeve," the giant grumbled, reaching into the teapot and scooping Josiah out onto the table. Josiah stood to his feet and watched as his huge captor unbuttoned his broadcloth shirt and flung it across the table in disgust. Josiah crept across to the garment, which was as big as a ship's mainsail. Sure enough, there was a four-foot tear in one of the sleeves.

"Insect, do you know how to mend a garment?" the giant suddenly boomed.

"Aye, sire, perhaps I could if I had a needle and thread," Josiah replied, afraid to admit that he had never before attempted such a task.

"I can't hear you," the giant complained. He plucked the boy from the table and deposited him in the iron kettle. "Do you mend?" he asked again.

"GET ME A NEEDLE AND THREAD AND I WILL TRY," Josiah shouted. The giant nodded his huge red head and left the room.

Moments later when the giant returned, he dropped a huge spool of thread and a four-foot pair of scissors into the pot beside Josiah. The boy stared at the thread, which was in reality a cord strong enough to hold a man's weight. A sewing needle the size of a dagger was tucked under the loops of cord.

"I want it finished by morning," the giant instructed Josiah, draping the torn sleeve into the kettle so that Josiah could reach it. "Indeed, it will go ill with you if the task is not completed by sunup."

As Josiah set about unwinding the cord from the spool, the Giant of Fear sat down and began to eat his dinner, which consisted of three whole roast pigs, twelve bushels of potatoes, and a small mountain of boiled greens. *He forgot that I haven't eaten since breakfast,* Josiah complained bitterly to himself. *He's so anxious to get his garment mended that—* Josiah paused and stared at the oversized thread. *This would be a perfect climbing rope. I could use this to climb down from the table!*

His heart began to throb with excitement as he thought about the possibilities for escape from the castle. *I'll wait till the giant is asleep tonight,* he told himself. *I'll keep working until he goes to bed, but as soon as he's asleep, I'll slide down the rope to the floor...*

The giant had turned from his dinner and was watching him closely, so Josiah hurriedly got on with the mending project. Lifting the huge scissors to an upright position, he struggled to open them.

Some hours later, all was quiet as Josiah crept across the castle floor. His heart pounded with fear and anticipation. The castle was dark, but the flames in the fireplace cast enough light across the room for him to see his way. The Giant of Fear was sound asleep in the next room; an occasional snore shook the floorboards of the castle. It had been a simple matter to tie a forty-foot length of the sewing line to the candlestick holder and slide safely to the floor. Now all he had to do was slip through the huge crack under the door and he would be free of the Castle of Unbelief once and for all.

Reaching the castle door safely, Josiah knelt and peered beneath the edge. His heart sank. The space beneath the massive door was nearly ten inches high, but the threshold under the door was at least six inches high, leaving a space of less than four inches.

There simply was not enough space to slip under the rough wooden door. Josiah was still a prisoner in the Castle of Unbelief, with no possible means of escape.

Chapter Sixteen

Discouragement swept over Prince Josiah as he studied the lower edge of the castle door. *There's not enough space to slide under the door like I thought I could,* he reasoned. *And the castle door is always locked, so there's no way that I can open it. What am I to do?*

He thought about the book so far above him on the mantle above the fireplace. *I will not leave the castle without the book, anyway. Perhaps the only thing to do is climb the line back to the table and finish the sleeve of the giant's jerkin before morning.* Discouragement overcame him; his shoulders sagged in defeat. There would be no escape from the Castle of Fear.

I must ask King Emmanuel for help, Josiah suddenly told himself. It was the first time since his capture by the Giant of Fear that the young prince had even thought of sending a petition to King Emmanuel. *I will never get out of this castle by myself, but perhaps my King will send help!* Determined now to send the petition, he began to search the castle for a parchment on which to send his plea for help.

He found a fragment of charred parchment on the hearth. Using a small piece of charcoal from the edge of the fire, he scrawled the following message:

"*To His Majesty, King Emmanuel,*

I have been captured by the Giant of Fear and have been held captive in the Castle of Unbelief for more than a week. I have tried to escape, but have found that by myself it is impossible. Please, Your Majesty, send help."

Not knowing whether or not he should use the title of "Prince", he simply signed the petition "Josiah". Rolling the fragment of parchment tightly, he opened his hand and watched as the petition shot across the room and disappeared through the wall of the castle. He immediately felt his fear begin to subside. *At least King Emmanuel will now know where I am,* he thought gratefully. *I just hope that he will receive my petition, even though I have failed him.* He crept across the vast floor of the Castle of Unbelief and took refuge in the shadows under the table.

"Use the Key of Faith," a gentle voice prompted, and Josiah glanced up in surprise.

There was just enough light from the fire for Josiah to make out the snowy form of the elusive white dove in the darkness overhead, perched on the back of one of the mammoth chairs. Josiah stared at the mysterious bird, and a wild idea popped into his head. "Did you speak?" he asked the dove. When there was no answer, Josiah shook his head. "No, of course you didn't speak." He dropped his shoulders and sighed. What was he to do?

"Use the Key of Faith," the voice urged again.

The Key of Faith! It was still in the book! What if the Key of Faith could unlock the door? Josiah stood and peered up at the lock, which was twenty feet above the floor. His sudden enthusiasm wavered. The keyhole was nearly big enough to insert his entire fist, but the Key of Faith was so tiny.

"Use the Key of Faith." The words were whispered this time, uttered so softly that Josiah barely heard them.

What was it that the Giant of Fear had said when he had first seen Josiah's Key of Faith? "Your faith is so small, it is hardly as big as a mustard seed."

The young prince paused, trying hard to recall a passage he had read in the book. It said something about having faith as small as a mustard seed and being able to move a mountain. *If faith like a mustard seed can move a mountain,* Josiah thought excitedly, *perhaps it can open a castle door!* Looking across the vastness of the great room, Josiah studied the immense wall beside the fireplace.

Forty feet. The mantle above the fireplace is about forty feet from the floor. If I can climb that wall, I can retrieve my book and my Key of Faith. And then, if the Key of Faith can open the castle door, I will be free again. Free to return to the Castle of Faith!

Listening intently for the occasional snores from the giant, Josiah hiked across the vast floor. He reached the fireplace wall safely, and tipping his head far back, looked at the mantel forty feet above him. *I can't escape the castle unless I can find a way to unlock the door,* Josiah told himself. *If I can climb the wall and reach the mantel, I can get my book back. And if the Key of Faith will open the castle door...well, I have to try!*

Josiah examined the rough stone wall. There were huge spaces between the stones that would afford him excellent handholds and footholds. Lifting his right foot high, he stepped up onto a projecting stone and then reached high for a handhold.

Three terrifying minutes later, he pulled himself up onto the mantel above the fireplace. Pausing to catch his breath and quiet his pounding heart, he looked over the edge. The flickering light of the fire illuminated the slate floor of the castle forty feet below him. He crept back from the edge and crawled across the mantel, afraid to stand to his feet. A thrill of joy filled his heart when he reached the book and picked it up.

Josiah clutched the precious book reverently to his chest for several long seconds and then hesitantly opened the cover. The Key of Faith was still there! Relieved, he carefully tucked the book under the length of line he had wrapped around his waist. His legs trembled and his heart was in his throat as he slowly backed over the edge of the mantel. Afraid to look down, he worked his way back down the wall, moving cautiously from stone to stone. A deep sigh of relief escaped his lips when he once again was standing safely on the floor.

The young prince hurried across the vast room, pausing to listen when he reached the shadow of the enormous table. A rumbling snore from the other room told him that the Giant of Fear was still asleep. Reassured that all was well, Josiah dashed across to the door of the castle.

The door latch was nearly twenty feet above him. Uncoiling the line from around his waist, Josiah quickly tied a slipknot and pulled open a wide loop. He hurled the line upward with all his might in an attempt to catch the loop around the latch, but his aim was off and the line came tumbling back to land in a pile at his feet. Coiling the line in loose loops, he tried again. On the fourth try, the loop dropped neatly over the latch and Josiah pulled the line, tightening the slipknot.

Prince Josiah opened the book and took out the Key of Faith. Holding the key between his lips, he grabbed the line and climbed hand over hand until he was at eye level with the keyhole. He wrapped his legs around the line. Gripping the line with his right hand, he took the tiny key from between his lips and inserted it into the huge keyhole.

To his astonishment, he heard a loud click, and the enormous castle door suddenly swung open. The Key of Faith had not only unlocked the door to the Castle of Unbelief; it had actually opened it. Josiah's heart throbbed with excitement as he slid down the line and leaped through the door. He was free! Faith had conquered fear and unbelief.

The morning sun was peeking over the hills to the east as the young prince trudged wearily up a gentle slope. He had been walking all night and now was tired, hungry and discouraged. The journey back to the Castle of Faith was taking so long. His weary steps took him over the crest of the hill, and he paused for a moment, drinking in the scene before him. "At last!"

The Village of Dedication lay just two or three furlongs in the distance, and just beyond, the Castle of Faith. The high stone walls of the castle glistened in the bright sunshine, warm and inviting. Josiah's heart beat faster, and he quickened his step. He was almost home.

"Prince Josiah!"

Josiah turned at the salutation. His heart leaped when he saw a minstrel dressed in green and gold seated at the base of a yew tree beside the path. "Encouragement!"

The cheerful minstrel rose to meet him. "I have been waiting for you, my prince. Pray tell, why did the journey take you so long?"

"I was delayed by the Giant of Fear," Josiah replied. "He had me imprisoned in the Castle of Unbelief for more than a week."

A sympathetic look crossed the minstrel's cheerful face. "I was aware that something like that could happen. I wish that I could have stayed with you. Fear often keeps Emmanuel's servants from reaching the Village of Dedication and the Castle of Faith. When we look at the obstacles and difficulties along the journey rather than trusting the promises of our King, the Giant of Fear can very easily take us hostage and even imprison us in the Castle of Unbelief."

Josiah drew the book from within his robe. "Do you know how I got out?"

"You have learned to use the Key of Faith," Encouragement replied with an understanding smile. "It is the only way." He took Josiah by the arm. "Come. I will accompany you to the Castle of Faith. A warm welcome awaits you."

Together the boy and the minstrel passed through the Village of Dedication. Josiah watched the townspeople as they went about their daily business, happy in the service of their King. An atmosphere of peace and contentment pervaded the busy streets of the little village. Josiah and Encouragement passed the tinsmith's shop and turned the corner, and the Castle of Faith once again came into sight.

Josiah wavered slightly as he walked up the approach to the drawbridge. What if Sir Faithful refused to allow him to enter the castle? What would he do if he were turned away because he had failed his King?

Encouragement noticed his hesitation and touched him gently on the arm. "Do not be anxious, Prince Josiah," he said softly. "There is nothing to fear."

"But I have failed. What am I to do if Sir Faithful or Lord Watchful will not allow me to enter the castle? What will I do if I am turned away?"

"Remember the words of your King. Trust in His promises."

"But what if—"

Encouragement placed two fingers on Josiah's mouth, interrupting him. "Say no more, Prince Josiah. Simply trust."

They had reached the edge of the drawbridge. Josiah's heart was pounding fiercely. Was he still a prince? Would he be allowed to return to the Castle of Faith as if nothing had happened, as if he had not failed his King? He would know within the next moment or two.

The castle gate swung open just then and a familiar figure hurried forward. "Sir Faithful!" Josiah ran to meet the old steward.

"Prince Josiah!" The old man's beard brushed Josiah's face as Sir Faithful's arms engulfed him in an exuberant hug. "Welcome home, lad."

Tears flowed down Josiah's cheeks and he trembled violently as he drew a breath and prepared to ask the question. "Sir Faithful?" His voice broke, and he tried again. "Sir Faithful, am I still a prince? Do I still belong to King Emmanuel?"

Sir Faithful stepped back and looked deeply into his eyes. A troubled look crossed his features. "My prince, why do you ask such a question?"

"I failed my King," Josiah replied, weeping. "I lost my sword, my ring, and my parchment! I failed to complete the mission for King Emmanuel. Tell me, Sir Faithful, am I still welcome in the Castle of Faith? I am not worthy."

The old steward regarded the trembling boy with sad eyes. "Josiah, Josiah. You have indeed failed your King. Argamor endeavored to distract you from His Majesty's business, and he was successful. Indeed, it is true that you are not worthy to be called by His Majesty's name, or to enter his castle."

Josiah's heart sank, and the tears flowed faster.

"But this was given to you by your King, and it is yours forever," Sir Faithful continued, handing Josiah a parchment. "Read it, Prince Josiah."

Josiah unrolled the parchment. "Be it known to all men everywhere," he read aloud, "that from this day henceforth and forever, Josiah Everyman, of the Village of Despair, has been adopted into the Royal Family of King Emmanuel and shall henceforth be known as Prince Josiah, heir eternal with King Emmanuel."

He looked up at Sir Faithful with tear-filled eyes. "It still says 'forever' and it still says 'eternal'. Does that mean that I am still a prince?"

The old man smiled as he put an arm around Josiah's shoulder. "It says 'forever', Prince Josiah, and that's what it means. King Emmanuel's signature and seal are still on the document, so you have His Majesty's word on it. Come; let us go into the castle. There is a joyous reception awaiting you."

Prince Josiah's heart was filled with joy as he walked side by side with Encouragement and Sir Faithful through the gates and into the Castle of Faith. A song of praise suddenly burst from his lips.

"I sing the greatness of my King, my Lord Emmanuel
His power is great and far exceeds
What mortal tongue or pen can tell.
My heart is full; I sing for him,
And trust that I may serve him well."

Glossary

Bailey: the courtyard in a castle.

Barbican: the space or courtyard between the inner and outer walls of a castle.

Battlement: on castle walls, a parapet with openings behind which archers would shelter when defending the castle.

Castle: a fortified building or complex of buildings, used both for defense and as the residence for the lord of the surrounding land.

Coat of arms: an arrangement of heraldic emblems, usually depicted on a shield or standard, indicating ancestry and position.

Crenel: one of the gaps or open spaces between the merlons of a battlement.

Curtain: the protective wall of a castle.

Doublet: a close-fitting garment worn by men.

Ewer: a pitcher with a wide spout

Furlong: a measurement of distance equal to one-eighth of a mile.

Garrison: a group of soldiers stationed in a castle.

Gatehouse: a fortified structure built over the gateway to a castle.

Great hall: the room in a castle where the meals were served and the main events of the day occurred.

Jerkin: a close-fitting jacket or short coat.

Keep: the main tower or building of a castle.

Lance: a thrusting weapon with a long wooden shaft and a sharp metal point.

Longbow: a hand-drawn wooden bow 5¹/₂ to 6 feet tall.

Lute: a stringed musical instrument having a long, fretted neck and a hollow, pear-shaped body.

Lyre: a musical instrument consisting of a sound box with two curving arms carrying a cross bar from which strings are stretched to the sound box.

Merlon: the rising part of a crenallated wall or battlement.

Minstrel: a traveling entertainer who sang and recited poetry.

Moat: a deep, wide ditch surrounding a castle, often filled with water.

Portcullis: a heavy wooden grating covered with iron and suspended on chains above the gateway or any doorway of a castle. The portcullis could be lowered quickly to seal off an entrance if the castle was attacked.

Reeve: an appointed official responsible for the security and welfare of a town or region.

Saboton: pointed shoes made of steel to protect the feet of a knight in battle.

Salet: a protective helmet usually made of steel, worn by knights in combat.

Scullion: a kitchen servant who is assigned menial work

Sentry walk: a platform or walkway around the inside top of a castle curtain used by guards, lookouts and archers defending a castle.

Solar: a private sitting room or bedroom designated for royalty or nobility.

Standard: a long, tapering flag or ensign, as of a king or a nation.

Stone: a British unit of weight equal to fourteen pounds.

Tunic: a loose-fitting, long-sleeved garment.

Trencher: a flat piece of bread on which meat or other food was served.

Castle Facts

- The first European castles were built as early as 950 A.D. They were made of wood.

- Stone castles were not built until around 1100 A.D.

- A castle could sometimes take as long as 20 years to build!

- Today it would cost several million dollars to build a typical castle.

- The bathrooms in castles were called garderobes.

- There are hundreds of castles still standing in Europe today.

- The moat around a castle was not always filled with water. Some moats were dry moats, but they were still effective in making it difficult for invaders to enter the castle.

- Inside a castle, the stairs usually circled upward to the right. This design made it easier for a right-handed castle defender to fight (standing on the stairs above his adversaries), by giving him more room to swing his sword.

- During the seventeenth century, gunfire made castles obsolete.